The millisecond the warmth of her mouth touched his, nothing else mattered.

Like it ever could.

The flat of his palm slapped against the door beside her head. Piper's leg wrapped high across his hip. Her fingers gripped his shoulders, pulling her body tighter against him.

Her lips parted beneath his, giving him the access he desperately craved. The taste of her flashed through him. And he wanted more.

Everything else in the world faded to nothing. Stone didn't care where they were. Who was close. Or what was going on around them. All that mattered was Piper and the way she was melting against him.

His fingers tangled in her hair. Her nails curled into his skin, digging in and leaving stinging half-moons. But her tiny, breathy pants made the bite insignificant.

He needed more of her.

* * *

The Rebel's Redemption by Kira Sinclair is part of the Bad Billionaires series.

Dear Reader,

It's no secret that I recently took a couple years away from writing. Circumstances have a way of derailing the best-laid plans and fate often enjoys proving no one can avoid unexpected events. No one understands that better than the three heroes in my upcoming Bad Billionaires series. All three men epitomize the idea that nothing, not even huge bank accounts, can prevent terrible things from sometimes happening. Working on these stories over the past year has been a gift. I absolutely fell in love with Stone, Finn and Gray. These three men definitely have a past, but with the right women by their sides, they might eventually find a future, too.

Anderson Stone has always been a bit of a rebel and from the time they were kids, Piper Blackburn's constant protector. He doesn't regret a single minute of the ten years he spent in prison defending her. Piper, on the other hand, couldn't be more angry with Stone. Oh, not for saving her, but for pushing her out of his life when they needed each other most. Once Stone is back in the family fold, it won't take long for Piper to confront him and the sparks to fly. Stone wants redemption, while all Piper needs is an explanation. However, going toe-to-toe with Stone will get her much more than she bargained for.

I hope you enjoy reading Stone and Piper's story as much as I enjoyed writing it! I'd love to hear from you at www.kirasinclair.com or come chat with me on Twitter at www.Twitter.com/kirasinclair. And don't forget to check out the other Bad Billionaires books coming soon!

Best wishes,

Kira

KIRA SINCLAIR

———

THE REBEL'S REDEMPTION

HARLEQUIN
DESIRE

HARLEQUIN®
DESIRE™

Recycling programs for this product may not exist in your area.

ISBN-13: 978-1-335-20936-8

The Rebel's Redemption

Copyright © 2020 by Kira Bazzel

This edition published by arrangement with Harlequin Books S.A.

For questions and comments about the quality of this book, please contact us at CustomerService@Harlequin.com.

Harlequin Enterprises ULC
22 Adelaide St. West, 40th Floor
Toronto, Ontario M5H 4E3, Canada
www.Harlequin.com

Printed in U.S.A.

Kira Sinclair's first foray into writing romance was for a high school English assignment, and not even being forced to read the Scotland-set historical aloud to the class could dampen her enthusiasm...although it definitely made her blush. She sold her first book to Harlequin Blaze in 2007 and has enjoyed exploring relationships, falling in love and happily-ever-afters since. She lives in North Alabama with her two teenage daughters and their ever-entertaining bernedoodle puppy, Sadie. Kira loves to hear from readers at Kira@KiraSinclair.com.

Books by Kira Sinclair

Harlequin Desire

Bad Billionaires

The Rebel's Redemption

Harlequin Blaze

The Risk-Taker
She's No Angel
The Devil She Knows
Captivate Me
Testing the Limits
Bring Me to Life
Handle Me
Rescue Me

Visit her Author Profile page at Harlequin.com, or kirasinclair.com, for more titles.

You can also find Kira Sinclair on Facebook, along with other Harlequin Desire authors, at Facebook.com/harlequindesireauthors!

I'd like to dedicate this book to my parents, Charles and Pat Follin. On more than one occasion they've been the steady rock and unfailing support in my life. Thank you! And I love you!

One

Ten years was a long time. But apparently not long enough to change a damn thing.

Nothing made that more evident than standing at the balustrade above his parents' ballroom, staring down at the crush of people milling about.

All of them waiting for a glimpse of him.

The only one of them he cared to see was the woman he needed to stay far away from.

Laughter floated up as the gawkers danced, drinking expensive champagne out of cut crystal flutes. Celebrating his return like he'd been tucked away on some private island for a decade instead of being incarcerated.

The glitz and glitter couldn't quite hide the maniacal flash of glee in their expressions. The blood-thirsty need for gossip.

As if he'd stand up here and orate some speech, spilling all the secrets he'd been protecting for years, simply because he was finally free.

Mocking amusement bubbled through his belly. Right. This whole evening was a farce, one with a terrible ending barreling straight toward him. Unfortunately, no amount of maneuvering could prevent what he knew was coming.

Anderson Stone, the prodigal son, was finally home, and everyone who was anyone in Charleston society had decked themselves out in their finest to scrutinize him and whisper politely behind his back.

At least in prison the enemy had been easy to identify. Here, everyone smiled to your face and then raked your reputation through the mud at the first opportunity.

"Darling, what are you doing up here? You should be down there. Your friends are anxious to welcome you home."

Turning, Stone took in his mother, still gorgeous even well into her sixties. Her dark hair had turned more silver in the last ten years and there were a few more wrinkles crinkling the edges of her eyes, but nothing—not even watching her son being led out of a courtroom in handcuffs—could dim the light behind her bright blue eyes. Or diminish the serene confidence of her smile.

Slipping up beside him, she offered her cheek for a kiss, which Stone would never consider refusing.

He'd put enough disappointment in her eyes. He'd do anything to avoid adding more.

But he didn't make any move toward the stairs that would lead him down into the pool of circling sharks. Instead, he gripped the sweating glass of Scotch tighter in his fist and leaned farther out over the railing.

"Sweetie," she murmured beside him, the heavy, comforting weight of her hand settling against his back. Who knew that at thirty, with all he'd seen and experienced, he could still need her touch to settle him like a toddler scared by a nightmare?

A scoffing sound scraped against his throat. He better than most was fully aware monsters didn't just live in dreams. And no comforting hand could soothe away reality, not even his mother's.

"I know you're struggling right now."

She had no idea, and he wasn't about to clue her in.

"But these people are here to support you."

Yeah, right. Stone couldn't help letting his gaze sweep across the crowd below. He had a hard time believing that, although he was reluctant to crush his mom's rose-colored view of the world by voicing his skepticism.

He'd been convicted of manslaughter, killing another member of their "set." It didn't matter that the bastard had deserved to die. Because only one other person knew that truth and he'd do absolutely anything to keep it that way.

Hell, he'd pleaded guilty and served time to keep the secret.

"Standing up here half the night isn't going to make it any easier."

God, on that, his mother was right. Pulling in a deep breath, Stone knocked back the rest of the Scotch in his glass, relishing the smooth taste of it across his tongue and the burn as it hit his gut. Good liquor was something he'd definitely missed.

Pushing away from the railing, he sent a forced smile in his mother's direction and hoped she wouldn't call him on the bullshit.

He was halfway to the staircase when her soft voice stopped him. "Anderson."

She was the only person in his life who'd ever called him by his given name. That sound in her lilting drawl had a twist of emotions storming through him—regret chief among them. Pausing, Stone turned back to look at her.

"I'm proud of you, son."

He had no idea how she could be, but she'd raised him right and he wasn't about to argue with her. Not now.

"There's plenty of time for you to figure out what you want to do next. I know your father offered you a position within the company, and we'd both be overjoyed if you accepted. But neither of us expect you to make that decision immediately. Take your time. Enjoy your freedom."

Stone nodded, not having the heart to tell her he really had no interest in joining Anderson Steel, named after his mother's grandfather. In a generation that rarely saw women in power positions in the business world, his parents had been jointly running the company as CEO and vice president since long before he'd been born.

His parents had met in the boardroom, going toe to toe when his own grandfather had brought in Nick Stone as a business consultant. Her Ivy League education newly minted, his mom hadn't taken kindly to being forced to accept an interloper's opinion. Or so the story went.

Sparks flew, but somewhere during compromising in the boardroom they'd ended up in the bedroom. And the rest was history.

Stone had always marveled at his parents' ability to work together all day and still manage to be so overtly in love with one another. Although in his preteen years he'd definitely gone through a phase of thinking their displays of affection were embarrassing as hell.

Anderson Steel was his parents' life, but he'd never felt as connected to it. He'd never wanted to join the company, although ten years ago it hadn't really occurred to him that he could choose a different path. Now…there was something about losing your freedom for ten years that made you rethink every simple decision in your life.

He was no longer willing to go along with what had been expected, especially since he knew Anderson Steel wasn't where he wanted to be. The problem was, he didn't have another path. Yet.

But he'd cross that bridge later.

One issue at a time.

His feet hadn't even hit the bottom step before the tasteful music drifting through the ballroom came to an abrupt stop. Every pair of eyes in the room turned, raking across him from head to toe.

Stone had no idea what they saw or thought. And, frankly, he didn't care.

No, that wasn't entirely true. One person there tonight mattered, even if she shouldn't.

He'd felt her the minute she entered the room. But he was going to do his best to ignore her presence, just as he was going to ignore the stares and whispers.

Piper Blackburn stood in the shadows. Her heart thumped painfully inside her chest and despite the glass of Merlot she'd just downed, her throat felt dry and scratchy.

She couldn't tear her eyes from him. Or stop her hands from shaking. Piper quickly deposited the empty glass on a nearby table before it slipped through her untrustworthy fingers.

The last thing she needed was to make a scene and draw his attention. Or, rather, she didn't want his attention yet. She needed to get a grip before she confronted him.

Before she unleashed ten years of pent-up frustration, hurt and guilt.

Her entire body quivered. Her skin felt flushed,

but an icy cold seeped into her veins. How was that possible?

Closing her eyes, Piper took several deep breaths, employing some of the calming techniques she taught her patients. Feeling a little more centered, she opened her eyes again. And immediately lost any sense of being centered when Stone was still in her line of sight.

Tall, strong and handsome as hell. He stood there, a dare to the room clearly filling those golden eyes.

He was different, but then she'd expected that. Ten years in prison would change anyone, right?

He was bigger. Not taller since even at twenty he'd been several inches over six feet, but broader. More muscular. Harder, not just in body, but in demeanor. The boy she'd known before had moved with easy grace. Oh, the grace was still there, but now it was like the silky outer shell covered up a core of pure steel.

Piper couldn't stop the bubble of hysterical laughter at her own joke. Steel for the son of the steel magnates. Seriously, she needed to get a grip or the speech she'd been working on was not going to come out the way she'd planned.

And that would piss her off more than anything.

Tonight might be Stone's return to society and freedom, but it was also going to provide closure. The last piece she needed to fully put the past behind her.

Slowly, murmurs began. People shifted. And then someone pushed through the crowd to clap Stone on the back and welcome him home. Hands propelled him forward through the crowd. For the better part of an hour Piper kept to the edges, watching as he greeted people he'd known his entire life with a blank expression that never shifted. He didn't smile or laugh. Stone was polite and confident, remote and untouched.

He was different and that was her fault.

However, that wasn't going to stop her from asking the questions she'd been denied answers to for ten years.

Piper waited, watching and biding her time. She refused the cold, frosted glasses of champagne several circulating waiters tried to entice her with. The last thing she needed right now was to be even more off-kilter.

When Stone cut through the crowd for his mother, leaned down and whispered something into her ear before heading for the stairs, Piper knew it was now or never. Her mouth went dry and for a moment she regretted not having one of the flutes so she could at least take a tiny sip. What she was about to do would be difficult if she couldn't find her voice.

With a deep breath, she skirted around the crowd, avoiding the main staircase Stone had used in favor of the smaller one tucked into the back of the room that the staff had been utilizing. Growing up, this house had been just as familiar as her own. Maybe more. She knew every nook and crevice. Had explored them with the man now trying to escape from the party thrown in his honor.

Escape her.

But Piper was done letting him ignore her.

The heavy wooden door at the top of the staircase opened onto the quiet hallway just in time for her to register the click of the library door closing at the far end. Of course he'd go there, the room where they'd spent so many hours together. The room filled with happiness and good memories.

As kids, they'd curl up on the rug in front of the massive fireplace and laugh as they read aloud to each other of wild and outlandish adventures. As teens, they'd lounged on the soft, tufted sofas, doing homework and philosophizing about the future.

Life had been so amazing, so wide-open with possibility.

And then it wasn't.

But not even that painful memory could stop her from opening the door and following him inside. Words, long practiced, swirled in her brain as the door snicked quietly closed behind her. Piper pressed her back against it, needing the support of the solid surface.

A warm, muted glow from a series of wall sconces washed the entire room in golden light. At the other end, Stone stood in front of the huge, curved windows, his back to her. Without even turning he said, "I wondered how long you were going to wait."

The heavy rumble of his voice scraped along all of her already jangling nerves. Electricity skipped across her skin. It was that simple and that complicated. Her reaction to this man had been a jumble of conflicting emotions for years.

Piper realized she was frozen like one of the ice swans that adorned the buffet downstairs when Stone twisted his neck, pinning her with a laser gaze. His remote expression was like a swift kick in the gut.

Asshole.

They'd been through too much for him to look at her with the same blank, dispassionate expression he'd given everyone else.

She deserved more from him, dammit.

Suddenly, she shot across the room, her long legs eating up ground as she raced toward him. All the words she'd practiced bubbled on her tongue, ready to spill out of her mouth.

Stone turned, his feet braced wide and his hands balled into the pockets of his perfectly tailored suit pants.

She wanted to slap him. To relish the sound of her hand cracking across that strong, stubborn jaw.

But she couldn't do it. Even angry, she was still so relieved to finally see him.

Instead, the momentum she'd gathered drove her straight into him. Her arms wrapped around his broad frame, plastering her body against him. Warmth and happiness and a churning regret settled deep in her belly.

Piper's eyes closed as a wave of yearning crashed over her.

It was so damn good to hold him.

And then she realized he hadn't moved. Stone's fists were still heavy balls tucked into the pockets of his pants. And his tall frame was as solid and unmoving as the wall behind them.

Embarrassment mixed with the anger that had initially propelled her forward.

She hadn't come here to throw herself at him.

Pushing away, she tried to find some space. "I'm sorry."

"For what?"

"I just watched two dozen people that don't really give a damn fawn all over you like you're the second coming of Christ, all while silently condemning them for being hypocritical and phony."

For a flash of a second a twinkle sparkled deep in his warm, tawny eyes. But it only lasted a breath before it was snuffed out. "That makes two of us."

"And I basically just did the same thing."

"Hardly."

Piper shook her head. "But it was either hug you or slap the hell out of you."

Stone's lush lips pulled down at the corners. "You're mad at me."

"Of course I'm mad at you, you nitwit." Great, now she was calling him names. She was breaking all the rules tonight. Why wouldn't she? She was dealing with Anderson Stone after all, the man known for thinking the rule book was nothing more than a suggestion.

"There's no reason."

Was he serious? "No reason? Stone, you refused

to see or speak to me for ten years. And after killing my stepbrother in order to protect me."

Sure, their relationship had been complicated back then, but they'd still been close. Best friends. And then he was just...gone.

When she'd needed him most.

But that wasn't what she was still angry about. She'd come to terms with what had happened. She'd spent years in therapy, getting the help she needed to work through her own anger and guilt. What she hadn't been able to let go of was the way he'd simply shut her out, refusing to let her protect him the way he'd always protected her.

"You didn't give me a chance, Stone. To admit that Blaine had been intimidating and harassing me for years before things escalated." Saying the words made the remnants of her own fury and regret spike. "You sacrificed everything, and then refused to talk to me."

Piper was so wrapped up in her own irritation that she didn't register the change in Stone's posture and expression until his hands wrapped around her upper arms, pulling her onto the tips of her toes so she could look him eye to eye.

"Harassing you for years?" The words were deadly, right along with the murderous expression just inches from her face. Unease skittered down Piper's spine and had her swallowing loudly in a useless attempt to get a grasp on the sudden turn of emotions.

Stone's words were measured and deliberate. "That wasn't the first time he'd hurt you?"

Slowly, Piper shook her head. "No. I mean, yes."

A low rumble rolled up through his chest, reminding her of a caged beast. One about ready to break free. "Which is it?"

"No, he hadn't sexually assaulted me before that night. But he'd hit me. Pinched me. Scared me. Once he cut me with a pair of scissors. But he pretended it was an accident and I couldn't prove it wasn't."

That history with Blaine was part of the reason she'd kept silent when she should have spoken up. Not only had everything happened so quickly that she hadn't really had time. But once she'd realized what Stone had done…she was afraid no one would believe her if she told the truth. Any evidence she'd had to support her claim against Blaine had been gone. She was afraid, hurt and lost. And uncertain that anything she had to say would make a difference.

Stone's fingers flexed around her biceps. He carefully lowered her until her feet were back flat on the ground. With deliberate care, his fingers unwrapped from her body, one by one. His hands brushed down her arms sending a cascade of tingles racing across her skin.

The softness of his touch was in such stark contrast to the harsh expression on his face. Piper wanted to touch him again. Instead, it was her turn to ball her hands into fists.

Scooting her to the side, Stone strode away from

her. Bewildered, Piper spun after him. "Where are you going?" They were far from done with this conversation.

Hands pressing into the ornate carvings on the door, Stone growled, "I want to dig up that asshole so I can pound his skull in again."

Piper's knees buckled. They just…failed her. One minute she was standing and the next she was a pile of arms and legs on the floor. Crap. Not exactly the picture of a powerful, successful woman she'd wanted to project.

She'd planned to show him she was strong now. Prove to herself, and him, that she was fine without him. Apparently, not true.

Stone's beautiful golden eyes went wide. His powerful body eating up ground, so she barely had time to pull a deep breath into her lungs before she was moving through the air, the world wobbling around her. But it righted again when she stopped, cradled against Stone's hard body.

The heady scent of him swirled around her. His warmth seeped into her skin, melting through her and making her already unsteady legs feel like jelly. Piper stared up at him, dazed and unsettled.

The harsh line of his mouth, pulled down at the corners, was so close. Right there. What was wrong with her that she wanted to close the miniscule gap between them and taste him?

It wasn't the first time she'd had the urge, but it had been a long time. So much for thinking she had complete control of herself.

Settling her onto the nearest sofa, a big leather monstrosity that was a heck of a lot more comfortable than it looked, Stone crouched in front of her. He stared at her for several seconds, his face so familiar and yet so foreign. Before she would have known exactly what he was thinking. Not only because they'd been so close she could practically finish his sentences, but because his expression had been so open she could read his emotions like one of the books on the shelves behind him.

Now there was nothing. No hint of what he thought or felt.

And for the first time since she'd planned this confrontation she stopped long enough to really wonder how their reunion made him feel.

No, that wasn't true. She'd thought about it and pushed away the only logical explanation she could come up with. He'd been so angry at her for what happened, for ruining his life—or so disgusted by what he'd seen that night—that he couldn't stomach the sight of her.

What she didn't understand was why he'd sacrificed his freedom and future for her if that was true?

Piper shook her head, unable to reconcile Stone's actions any more now than she had then, or over the last ten years.

Stone was the first to break contact, settling his gaze on her shoulder. The sleeveless couture gown she was wearing had a high collar that wrapped around her throat and a subtly sexy keyhole that left a large part of her spine naked. His gaze followed the line of her arm that was draped across the curve of her hip.

The deep pink flat of his tongue slipped across his mouth as his gaze traveled down her body. His fingers followed, rough and warm when they ghosted over her shoulder and down the line of her arm. Barely there, the touch was a whisper and shouldn't have been enough to ignite a flame deep inside.

But then her body had never responded right when Stone was around. At least, not since she was fifteen.

"Why didn't you ever say anything?"

Piper shrugged. "What could I say? You know Blaine was a brat from the day I moved in."

Stone's face went hard again, shutting off in a way that made her fingers jerk with the need to touch him. Soothe him. But that wasn't her right.

"There's a huge difference between being a prick and physically harming you, Piper." Stone's voice dripped with irritation.

"I'm well aware of that, Stone," she snapped. "It's not like it was constant. Things would be okay, as okay as they ever could be with Blaine, and then out of the blue he'd just pass me in the hallway and punch me hard enough to leave a bruise. But never where anyone else would see."

"You should have said something."

She shrugged. "So you could do what? If I'd ever thought he'd go so far… I would have. But I was almost free. A couple more months and I would have been out of the house and away from him."

She'd often wondered if that was what had set him off—changed things—that night. It was a question she'd never get the answer to.

Piper waved her hand, brushing the topic away. "There's no point in rehashing any of that." She'd spent years in therapy and had come to a sense of peace where Blaine was concerned.

What she needed now was closure with Stone. To move past the craving she'd spent years trying to convince herself didn't exist.

She'd walked into this room angry with him—and herself—but underneath all of that had always lived a bubbling well of yearning and bewilderment. Now, staring into his golden eyes, she had the overwhelming urge to find some way to finally purge it.

"I'm sorry," she said, the words out of her mouth before she even realized she wanted to say them.

"For what?"

For what? How could he not know? "For ruining your life."

Two

Piper's soft words slammed into him like a fist to the chest. But she kept talking, completely unaware of the impact.

"I've worked hard to move past what Blaine did to me. He doesn't have any power over me anymore."

Thank God. Stone's hands, now balled into fists on his thighs, flexed against the need to touch her again. But he couldn't allow himself that luxury. Didn't deserve it.

"What I can't get past is what *you* did to me."

And that, right there, was why he couldn't touch her.

Because he didn't blame her for hating him. He hated himself for the way things went down. Not that he would have changed a damn thing.

Not if it meant Piper was safe.

Only years of practice at keeping a tight lid on everything inside allowed Stone to regain his blank expression. But her words pierced his flesh just the same. Hurting worse than the stab wound he'd gotten his first year behind bars. Before he'd figured out how to amass power, fear and respect.

Out of nowhere, her palms landed flat on his chest as she shoved at him. Under normal circumstances he could have stayed balanced on the balls of his feet, but this entire situation was far from normal. Rocking backward, Stone found himself sprawled on his ass, staring up at Piper.

The complete absurdity of the entire situation hit him all at once. Laughter rolled through him, the sound rusty even to his own ears. If Finn and Gray could see him right now they'd be laughing their asses off, too. Closing his eyes, he stopped fighting it all and just collapsed, sprawling haphazardly across the soft rug beneath him.

God, even that felt amazing.

"Stop it." Piper's incredulous voice called him back to reality. Reluctantly, Stone opened his eyes, staring into her disbelieving expression. "Nothing about this is funny."

"Oh, you're wrong." On so many levels. "Very wrong." Everything about the situation was funny.

Rolling, Stone pushed up from the ground. Another bubble of amusement tickled the back of his throat as Piper's expression morphed from irritation to wariness. He'd always said she was a smart woman.

Putting several feet between them, Stone moved to the other side of the room again, shoving his fists back into his pockets. Maybe then they'd stop itching to touch her again.

"Plenty of men bigger and stronger than you have tried to put me on my ass. You don't find it funny that a woman who barely tops one-twenty managed to do what they couldn't? Because I do."

Her mouth flattened, drawing his attention in a way he had no doubt she was oblivious to. "I've had plenty of hand-to-hand combat training."

That sobered him up quickly. Because there was no mistaking what had prompted her to get that training.

"So have I." His, however, had been learned the hard way.

When he'd first agreed to the plea bargain, his attorney had assured him that he'd be taken to a minimum-security prison. The kind of place they kept white-collar criminals. But white-collar criminals were still criminals. And none of them particularly cared to have a murderer among them. Especially a notorious one they felt had bought his way into a lesser sentence.

It didn't help that the story of Blaine's death and his own speedy conviction had hit all the major networks. His tight-lipped refusal to speak to anyone about what happened added fuel to the fire. Sensationalizing the story in a way that everyone, including his lawyers, PR people and even his parents, had pleaded with him to do something to defuse. But he'd refused to speak to anyone about the truth, letting his lawyer say only that it had been accidental. It had taken months for the reporters to stop pestering him.

"Why'd you do it?"

A harsh sound scraped through Stone's throat. He knew exactly what she was asking, but chose to feign misunderstanding.

"Kill him? I should think that was obvious. Actually, I didn't intend to kill him, which is what saved me from a murder charge."

He should have known Piper wasn't going to let him get away with the subterfuge though. She always had been quick to call him on his bullshit.

"You know that's not what I meant. Why'd you take the plea? Why didn't you let me tell the police the truth? They didn't even question me. What did you tell them? Why did you refuse to see me, talk to me?"

With each word, Piper's voice escalated until it was bouncing off the lined shelves surrounding them. If she didn't watch it, everyone downstairs would hear her and all those years he'd spent locked away would be for nothing.

As he stalked toward her, intending to simply tell her to hush, the flash of fear she immediately banked didn't go unnoticed. He stopped a few inches away. Still close enough to feel her warmth coming off that luscious body in caressing waves that made his blood simmer.

"It wouldn't have changed anything."

"That's bull," she hissed. "It could have changed everything. You were defending me."

"I killed him." He'd taken another life, plain and simple. "There was no reason for you to recount the horror that he'd inflicted on you, *in front of his father and your mother,* because it didn't matter."

"It mattered to me."

Not enough for her to go—

Nope, he wasn't going to finish that thought. He hadn't wanted her to come forward. Hadn't wanted her to endure any more pain.

"And then you just…cut me off. You were my best friend, Stone. My person. The one I told everything to."

"Not everything," he couldn't stop himself from saying.

Piper flinched, her nostrils flaring on a heavy breath.

"Why wouldn't you let me visit you? Be there for you, the way you were for me."

There was no comparison. And no way he would have allowed Piper to see him the way he'd been those first few months, bruised and halfway to broken. He'd also refused to see his mother, although he didn't expect Piper knew that. The only person he'd allowed to visit was his father, and only because he'd extracted a promise that he wouldn't tell anyone about the state Stone was in. Reluctantly, his father had agreed, realizing it was something he couldn't fix for his son and that Stone was going to have to figure out how to deal with the situation himself.

It was the first time his father had treated him like a man instead of a boy. Maybe it was the first time he'd actually been a man instead of a boy.

"Look, Piper. You had no business anywhere near that place."

"Neither did you," she gritted out, her entire face pinched with unhappiness and sorrow.

Stone shrugged. "It's over. History. No reason to dissect what happened."

She shook her head, a small gust of laughter that held not an inch of humor dripping from her lips. "Dissecting the past is what I do for a living as a psychologist, or weren't you aware of that?"

He knew exactly what she'd been doing with her life. His father had given him monthly updates on everyone who mattered.

"Fine, even if I give you that one, which for the record I don't agree with your reasoning, what about the letters I wrote that you returned? What about them, hmm?"

Stone tried not to notice the way her crossed arms beneath her breasts thrust them higher against the tight material of her gown. Or the way the shiny, slithery fabric clung to the curve of the hip she'd popped out in exasperation. The half-hard erection that sprung up was highly inconvenient.

And if he was a weaker man, he might try to convince himself that his physical reaction to Piper had more to do with the length of time he'd been without the soft curves of a woman's body. But that would be a lie and he tried very hard never to lie, especially to himself.

His reaction had everything to do with the woman in front of him, because he'd been fighting it since she was around sixteen. It had been just as troubling then since doing anything about it would have not only been inappropriate, but would have jeopardized the friendship that had meant so much to him. And after…he hadn't deserved her. Still didn't.

Shifting his feet, Stone tried to find a couple extra inches in the tailored tux pants, but the damn things felt like they were strangling him no matter how he moved.

"Stone!"

Right, letters. "I didn't want to read them, so I sent them back." Maybe if he hadn't currently been in the throes of torture he'd have found a subtler way of responding. The stricken expression on Piper's face hurt to watch, but when she turned from him, he realized his straightforward response might be a better solution to his problem in the long run.

He'd known from the minute he walked through the front door to his parents' estate that he would have to face Piper. She obviously had questions and plenty of anger to direct his way. And he'd been dreading it for days.

A small part of him had hoped the distance that had grown between them would keep her away. But he knew her well enough to realize that wasn't a possibility. Aside from the apparently continued harassment by her stepbrother, he'd never known Piper not to meet any challenge head-on.

It's one of the things he'd admired most about her back then and there was no reason to think she'd changed so drastically since.

Perhaps his words were the single punch that would put them both out of their misery and end the torture. Because no matter what, he couldn't have Piper in his life.

Even if she didn't see a monster when she looked at him…he did. And not just because of what he'd done to Blaine. It was everything he'd done since then, too. And everything he hadn't. His life had stalled ten years ago while Piper's had flourished. She'd become successful. She'd fought against the aftereffects of what she'd gone through.

And he was so proud of her for that.

But he didn't want to be a constant reminder to her and he had no idea how to prevent that. How could she be in the same room with him and not flash to that night?

So, he'd come to the conclusion that Piper had been through enough and he couldn't be the source of more pain for her.

Unfortunately, hurting her right now was the best way to prevent more misery later.

His words lanced through her, although it was nothing more than she'd expected. What other explanation could there be? Obviously, he blamed her for his life going to hell. Stone never would have been in that prison if it wasn't for her.

Shaking her head, Piper tried to breathe through the tightness in her chest. Losing her composure right now wouldn't help. For several seconds, she stared at Stone.

What the hell was she doing?

She wasn't sure anymore what she'd hoped to accomplish by forcing this conversation.

No, that wasn't true. She'd wanted to see him with her own eyes. She'd *needed* to see him. To know if the craving was still there.

And, dammit, it was.

She'd lied to herself, convincing her gullible mind that she'd wanted nothing but closure. Not the fantasy that he'd take one look at her, scoop her into his arms and kiss the hell out of her, confessing he'd always wanted more.

Unfortunately, it was clear that fantasy had been hers alone. Stone had never given her any indication he wanted anything other than friendship from her.

So, in the end, closure was what she was going to get. There was nothing between them to revive, not even the friendship.

Forcing words past the uncomfortable lump in her throat, Piper said, "Hearing you say that hurts. But I understand and I won't bother you anymore."

Gritting out a sickly smile, she started to push past him, her only thought to reach the door and get out before all the emotions roiling inside her erupted in an embarrassing bout of tears. The last thing she wanted Stone to see was her vulnerability.

Her vision tunneled down to the ornate door in front of her. Escape. Which was why she wasn't prepared to hold back the involuntary gasp when the hot, heavy weight of his hand wrapped around her upper arm and jerked her still.

"Piper." The single low word scraped across her nerves, making her scalp prickle.

He held her still, his body crowding close without actually touching her. She purposely kept her gaze pointed away from him when she asked, "What do you want from me, Stone?"

Her heart raced, thumping so hard she was certain he could hear it in the heavy silence that stretched between them. He didn't move, not even a twitch of his fingers around her bicep. The seconds ticked by and that tingle cascaded down her spine, energizing and uncomfortable all at once.

When she couldn't take it anymore, Piper finally cut her gaze to the side and looked at him. And what she saw staring back had everything inside her stilling. Such anger, despair and hope filled his dark, tawny eyes. She wanted to reach out and brush her fingers across his face. To soothe him at the same time she assured him everything would be okay.

But that wasn't her place.

"I don't want anything from you, Piper."

"Then let me go."

Now his fingers flexed and she thought he was

going to do exactly what she'd asked. Instead, his grip tightened.

His lips parted, but she never found out what he would have said because her smart watch thumped against her wrist. Suspended midair between them, the glowing light of the awakened screen drew their attention. The tension between them snapped when their gazes disconnected.

But anxiety of a different sort blasted through her when she read the words scrolling across the small screen.

I'd like to talk about your brother's death. Give me a call so we can set up a time for you to tell your side of the story.

Piper's whole body went cold at the same time a clammy sweat popped up across every surface of her skin. The last thing she wanted to do was speak to a reporter about Blaine.

She'd come to terms with what had happened, but that didn't mean she wanted to talk to someone who would tell the world. And there was no question that's exactly what would happen if she met with a reporter.

This wasn't the first one who'd contacted her in the last couple months with questions about Stone and Blaine.

Ten years ago, she'd been nothing more than a footnote to the story since Blaine's death had happened at her graduation party. No one had linked her to what had happened. Not really. There'd been plenty of speculation—a woman, drugs, a business venture gone bad—but no one had considered she might actually be at the center of the controversy surrounding the scandal. Which had worked in her favor.

Now the vultures were looking for any morsel of information they could take to turn Stone's release into a national sound bite.

"What the hell?" His deep voice hardened even as he jerked her arm closer so he could get a better look at the words on her wrist. Piper didn't even attempt to regain control of her arm, but let his movements pull her closer to him.

It was selfish, and she'd regret it later, but she was weak enough to soak in the warmth of him while she could get it.

Stone's already drawn mouth tightened even more. "Want to explain?"

"Not particularly."

Letting out a grunt, Stone said, "Start talking anyway."

Piper shrugged. "Reporters have been bothering me for months."

"Why am I just now hearing about this?"

"I don't know…because you've refused to talk to me for ten years and I didn't think you'd give a damn?"

Raking long fingers through his hair, Stone paused to pull at the ends as if he wanted to rip it out by the roots. His obvious frustration shouldn't have restored her sense of equilibrium, but it did.

There was something soothing about seeing him as off-kilter as she'd been feeling.

But that was a petty reaction, so Piper pushed it away.

"This doesn't have anything to do with you, Stone."

"The hell it doesn't."

"Not really."

Stabbing a finger in the direction of her wrist, he said, "That's your private number, Piper."

"I'm well aware of that."

"How'd they get it?"

Crossing her arms over her chest, Piper tried not to let his words cause a reaction she couldn't control. "I'm easy to find. The nature of my business means I need to be accessible."

A sound that resembled a growl rolled through Stone's chest. It had Piper rocking back on her heels for a second. God, the man was infuriating and confusing.

"A few minutes ago, you were in the process of kicking me out of your life permanently, so let's just pretend you didn't see that text and go back to me walking out that door."

"That text changes things."

Raising a single eyebrow, Piper said, "It changes nothing." She spun on her heel intending to leave, suddenly needing space. "I don't owe you anything, least of all an explanation about what's happening in my life right now."

Piper's hand landed on the doorknob, but before she could twist and jerk, the flat of Stone's palm connected with the surface, a loud smack reverberating through the air between them.

He crowded into her personal space, applying pressure against the door so it didn't budge when she pulled.

"That may be true, but we're going to talk about this anyway."

Throwing him a glare over her shoulder, she said, "Or what?"

"Or I'm going to toss you over my shoulder and lock you in a room until your temper cools."

"Good luck with that."

"Try me, Piper. I murdered someone to keep you safe. You don't think I'm above some high-handed tactics to ensure you stay that way?"

His tone seemed to indicate he thought what he'd done was terrible. But Piper wouldn't ever be able to think of him as a murderer, or as anything other than her savior that night.

Suddenly, she just felt tired. Exhausted down to her bones. It had been an emotional few days. She couldn't remember the last night she'd slept the whole way through. It had been weeks, maybe months.

"It's just a reporter, Stone. I'm perfectly capable of ignoring whomever it is."

Stone shifted behind her, the open lapels of his jacket brushing against her back. The overwhelming urge to just lean into him and let him infuse her with his strength was difficult to deny. But somehow she found the will to ignore it.

Scooting sideways, Piper dipped under his

arm and away from the tempting heat of him. She straightened her shoulders, purposely tipped her chin up and with measured steps walked back to the chair she'd been sitting in before.

When chaos was swirling around her, the one sure way to maintain her calm was to control the things she could—like her posture and actions.

"What do you want to know?"

"You said reporters have been contacting you for months. Why?"

Piper tilted her head to the side and gave him an "are you serious" look. "I don't know, Stone. Maybe because with your release everyone is interested in the story again."

"I know that. The PR group at Anderson Steel has been fielding inquiries daily. I meant why *you*. Why now? They left you alone before."

Piper opened her mouth to make some smart-ass answer, but stopped herself when his words actually registered. Snapping her lips together, she studied him for several seconds, narrowing her gaze as she watched him.

"How do you know that?" she finally asked, each word slow and precise.

"How do I know what?"

"That they left me alone before."

"Dad told me."

"Because you asked or because he was just imparting information?"

His jaw tightened and for a second she thought he wasn't going to answer her. "Because I asked."

Piper stared at him, unsure what to make of that confession. She wanted to ask him, but was afraid he wouldn't give her an honest answer. Or that she wouldn't like what he said.

"My guess is they're fishing. I was of little consequence before because I was an eighteen-year-old kid. Now, I'm a successful adult. With a psychology degree. Not only could they get insider information, they could also get an expert with a professional opinion."

"You're not talking to them."

It irritated her that there wasn't a question mark at the end of his statement. "You're hardly in a position to be issuing orders."

His hands went to his hair again, tugging. Apparently, he'd picked up a new habit since she'd last seen him. One that surfaced when he was frustrated.

"Please, then. Don't talk to them."

Suddenly, the exhaustion was back. A wall that she couldn't push through anymore. Shrugging, she said, "Why would I?" It was easy to give him what he wanted considering that's what she'd planned to do anyway.

Finding her feet, Piper pushed up from the chair. With precise steps, she crossed the room. "Well, this night hasn't gone as planned. I'm going home."

"No, you're not. We're not finished with this conversation."

Giving him the ghost of a smile, she reached for the door. "Watch me."

Three

For the second time that night, Stone stood at the balustrade looking out over the crowd of people below. Only this time he had a purpose other than procrastination.

His gaze was glued to Piper as she maneuvered through the people they'd known their whole lives. She stopped and smiled, talked and laughed. Acted as if the last half hour hadn't even happened.

Part of him marveled at how completely she could keep herself together while he was struggling not to punch a fist-sized hole in the wall behind him.

Honestly, he wasn't certain which part of their conversation had him more upset. Hurting her feelings had been more unpleasant than he'd ever expected. It was one thing to know he was going to have to do it, but another to see the pain flickering deep inside her pale blue eyes and know he was the cause.

"So, as bad as you expected?" Gray Lockwood asked as he slipped up beside Stone. Draping his arms over the banister, Gray mirrored Stone's stance, staring down into the swirling people below, and waited. They'd both gotten pretty damn good at waiting.

"Worse."

Gray laughed, the sound carrying a self-deprecating edge to it. "Yeah. Tell me about it. At least your people threw you a party. My family wants nothing to do with me."

"That sucks, man."

He, Gray and Finn had met in prison and after a few rocky moments, had become closer than friends. They were brothers, and had spent the last several years watching each other's backs. Gray had been the first of them to be released, about eleven months ago, after serving a sentence for embezzling forty million dollars from the family company. Which was laughable considering the guy was worth at least half a billion without the company money. Even after paying back twenty mil, which Gray swore he didn't actually steal, he still had enough mad money to buy and sell several developing countries.

The courts had only been able to seize the assets needed as evidence, those they could prove were gained as a result of the crimes or what was needed for reparation. So, they'd all been able to keep most of their wealth.

Gray shrugged. "It is what it is. I've made my peace with it."

His friend might have convinced himself that he had, but Stone still heard the bitterness he couldn't quite hide.

"It gets easier," Gray promised.

Well, that was a relief.

"Good, because if every day on the outside is like this, I think I'd rather be back in."

Gray spun, pressing his back to the railing, and tossed him a wry grin. "Bullshit."

"Yeah, you're right."

"You gonna tell me who the beautiful woman in the killer dress is?"

Stone knew exactly who he was talking about, but decided to play dumb anyway. "There are lots of beautiful women down there. Be more specific."

"Maybe, but there's only one you've been staring at like you expect her to impersonate a magician's rabbit and disappear at any second."

"Ha! Where do you come up with this?"

"Stalling will not work here, man."

"She's no one important."

"So you wouldn't mind if I went down there and asked her to have dinner with me?"

There was no explaining the rush of possessive anger that overwhelmed him. "She's off-limits, Gray."

"Hmm. That's what I thought. Let me guess. Piper?"

He could lie, but there was no point. Gray could

find out who she was if he wanted and the moment Stone made a big deal out of this his friend would start digging.

"Yeah."

"Is she responsible for the combination of anger, irritation and kicked puppy filling your expression?"

Dammit, he'd thought he had his mask in place. Apparently not. Or maybe Gray just knew him well enough to see beneath it. He could lie, but there was no use. "Yeah."

"I assume the reunion didn't go well."

"Let's just say it ended with her pissed and storming out of the room." Which was what he'd wanted, right? So why did he feel like a combination of a complete ass and that kicked puppy?

"What did you say to her?"

"Nothing that didn't need to be said."

Shaking his head, Gray bounced on his heels. "Have I mentioned that you're an ass?"

"Not lately."

"Well, you are."

"Doesn't matter anyway. My plan was to leave her alone, but that's not an option anymore."

"Why not?"

"Because she's too stubborn to realize she's putting herself in harm's way."

"You realize she's not your responsibility, right? You're not required to slay every dragon in her life, man. She's too beautiful to be alone. Let whoever's occupying her bed take care of the problem."

Stone was just as surprised as Gray when he

found his fists twisting Gray's crisp white shirt.
"Don't make snide comments about her like that
again."

Gray held up his own hands in the universal sign
for surrender. "Message received, man."

Jesus, what was wrong with him? His temper
hadn't been on this much of a hair trigger since his
first year or so behind bars. When he'd learned to
control his responses. But the suggestion of Piper
in bed with someone else…his brain had short-
circuited.

Because he wanted to be the man sleeping next to
her and he couldn't be. Didn't deserve to be.

Easing up, Stone blew out a breath. "Sorry."

"My fault. Besides, I pushed the button on purpose."

"Because you're an asshole."

"Because I'm your friend and I'm worried about
you. But why don't we postpone the transition-to-
the-real-world conversation and concentrate on what
changed with your girl."

"She's not my girl."

"Sure, she isn't."

Shaking his head, Stone swallowed back the re-
tort on his tongue. It wouldn't do any good. Gray
was a hardheaded prick. "The media has been pestering her, too, apparently."

"Not surprising."

Gray's immediate reaction surprised Stone. "Really? I didn't expect it. They left her alone before."

"They're fishing, Stone." Gray leaned farther

back so he could snag Stone's gaze. "You know how to stop that."

"Not happening, man."

His friend shrugged. "Yeah, I know, but I wouldn't be your friend if I didn't say it. Again."

He really wished everyone around him would let it go.

"So, what do you want me to do?"

"Who says I want you to do anything?"

Gray laughed, the sound deep and slow. "Because I know you, buddy, and you can't let well enough alone. It's one of your best qualities and biggest flaws."

Stone flipped him off, but didn't argue. Because his friend wasn't wrong.

"I want to know more about the reporter who texted Piper. I don't like the fact that she's so exposed. She has no regard for protecting herself."

Gray's head turned. Stone didn't need to follow in order to know his friend was watching Piper below them. "I don't know, man. She looks pretty capable of taking care of herself to me."

Maybe, but old habits died hard.

"Information, that's all. You better than most know how valuable and powerful it can be."

Gray made a humming sound in the back of his throat. "And now you have a purpose. One that's more intriguing than the thought of stepping into the executive offices at Anderson Steel."

The problem with having friends who knew everything about him was that they didn't hesitate to use the knowledge against him at the most inconvenient times.

"Maybe."

"No maybe about it, counselor. Or maybe CEO? Which one of the many degrees you managed to amass during your time behind bars are you actually planning to use, hmm?"

Stone registered Gray's jab. It was one he liked to throw whenever he could. "Look, man, just because you're jealous that I'm smarter than you doesn't mean you need to be a prick."

"Actually, I kinda think it does. We both know you're like a hamster without a wheel when you don't have a goal or a project—sad and somewhat dangerous. I'm just saying this gives you something to focus on. At least for the moment. And you're in luck. I'm also at loose ends these days and could use a distraction. So, you have a team of two."

"Oh, goody."

Despite the sarcasm, Stone was happy to have Gray's help. He was going to protect Piper, whether she wanted him to or not.

Piper slipped the key into the lock on her house and twisted. She was so looking forward to kicking these heels off and stripping out of the bra currently digging into her ribs. Collapsing into bed sounded like heaven, too.

After everything, she was just bone-tired.

But that plan evaporated when she walked into her kitchen to find her best friend sitting at her table.

An open bottle of wine and an empty glass sat in front of her. Another glass stalled halfway to her own lips.

Part of her wished Carina wasn't there, but the rest of her could really use the comforting support Carina would no doubt give her. Out of everyone, she might be the only person to really understand how draining tonight had been. Which, given the circumstances, would probably appear weird to anyone on the outside looking in. But that was her family, twisted and complicated.

The petite blonde didn't even ask before pouring a healthy glass of wine and holding it in her direction.

"You survived."

"Barely." Piper shook her head at the same time she kicked her heels across the room. She should feel remorse for abusing her favorite pair of Louboutins, but right now she didn't. "Let me change first."

Her home was small, but it was perfect for her. The caretaker's cottage was located on the back of her mother and stepfather's estate. A couple years ago, after she'd graduated with her PhD, she'd tried to move out and into her own place, but her mom wouldn't hear of it. She insisted the house would simply sit vacant if Piper left. And that she was doing them a favor by staying. Besides, it made her mother feel better to have her close. And she did have her privacy. With her own drive onto the property, she could go days without seeing her parents if she wanted to. And there was the perk of having access to their heated pool whenever she wanted.

She'd relented and stayed. She did love the place. It was perfect for her, small and quaint, made of gorgeous stone. She had her own garden out back that provided her a place of tranquility when she needed it most. It worked.

And, it helped that Carina lived on the property, too, in the pool house.

Piper peeled off her gown and donned a pair of cotton shorts and a T-shirt so soft and comfortably worn. That's what she needed right now, comfort.

Padding back into the kitchen on bare feet, she scooped up the chilled glass and took a huge gulp. The sweetness of the Riesling exploded across her tongue. With a sigh, she collapsed into the kitchen chair Carina toed out for her. Pulling her legs beneath her, Piper rested her chin on one knee.

"That good, huh?"

She just shook her head, unsure where to even start to share her night with her friend. Because it was more complicated than simply her own emotional issues with Stone.

Carina had been her stepbrother's fiancée. Since she was several years older than Piper, they hadn't been particularly close before Blaine's death. But afterward, her parents had taken Carina in. She'd been devastated and alone in the world. Piper was fairly certain her stepfather had chosen to take care of Carina because he was trying to hold on to a piece of his son. But over the last decade, Carina had become family as much as she would have if she and Blaine had gotten married.

And, to be honest, floundering with her own emotional turmoil, and lost without Stone, Piper had needed a friend and Carina had been there for her. They'd become close, sharing in their grief, even if the emotion flowed from different sides of the experience.

She'd never confided the truth of what had happened to Carina. She just couldn't shatter Carina's view of Blaine. Adding to her friend's pain would serve no purpose.

Reaching across the table, Piper grasped Carina's hand. "Let's table my night for a second. We can go back to that, but right now I want to know how you're doing." After all, her fiancé's murderer had just been released from prison.

Carina gave her the ghost of a smile. It was all Piper had been getting from her friend for months, not that Piper blamed her.

"I'm okay."

"Really?"

Her pale blond hair swished around her face as she shook her head. "I'm as good as anyone can expect, let's put it that way? It's hard not to be angry."

"Which is normal, Carina. I'd be worried about you if you weren't upset. The important thing is being aware of your reaction, recognizing the things that trigger the emotion and channeling it in a healthy manner."

"Yes, Doctor." Carina gave her a wry grimace.

"Sorry." Sometimes it was difficult for her to turn

off work mode, especially lately with her friend. Carina was important to her and she wanted to help.

Carina flipped her hand, gripping Piper's and giving her a quick squeeze. "No, I know you mean well."

"I do."

"There's a part of me that will always carry anger toward Stone, but I understand your relationship with him is more complicated than mine. You were so close for so long."

"Maybe, but we're not anymore." And they hadn't been for a while. Tonight had proven that to her, even if the last ten years hadn't. Stone was a different person, harder. And she no longer knew him the way she had before he'd gone away.

It was clear Stone didn't want her in his life now. And she had to respect his wishes. That was the right thing to do.

"We talked. I don't know that I got the closure I was looking for, but I'm pretty sure I got all I'm going to get from him." It was her turn to shake her head. "I'm just going to have to learn to live with it and figure out how to move past it all."

She was also going to have to learn how to let go of this longing for him.

"Easier said than done," Carina murmured.

Piper whispered, "Yeah.

"But that wasn't all that happened tonight. That reporter texted me again."

"I thought you told her you weren't interested."

"I did," Piper replied, "but she's persistent. I

wouldn't worry about it, except Stone saw the text and was not thrilled."

"I bet." Carina's voice dripped with sarcasm.

"Carina."

Her friend shook her head. "I'm sorry. I just… wish I could understand what happened, Piper."

"I know." Although, if Piper had her way Carina would never learn the truth. While she didn't normally advocate lying, in this instance the truth could do nothing but hurt her friend and the memory she had of the man she loved…even if not entirely accurate. "He isn't going to talk."

Of that, Piper was absolutely certain. Stone had made his stance perfectly clear. She might not know him well anymore, but she had no doubt he meant every word and had no intention of ever changing his mind.

"I know," Carina sighed. "What are you going to do?"

Piper dropped her cheek to her knees. "Right now? I'm going to finish this glass of wine and then head to bed. Tomorrow, I'm going to call Ms. Black's boss and threaten harassment charges if she doesn't leave me alone."

Four

Stone's fist tightened around the edges of his phone. The plastic creaked, threatening to give beneath the pressure of his hold.

"Dude, let up before you break that shiny new piece of technology you just bought."

"I don't care," he gritted out between his clenched teeth. He could buy a thousand more. What he cared about right now was the picture filling every pixel of the screen.

Turning to face the two men on the other side of the room, Stone asked, very precisely, "How did this happen?"

He wanted to yell, but that wouldn't accomplish anything. He wanted answers more and that wasn't likely to happen if everyone around him was flinching from a display of temper.

Mitchell, his father's head of security, spoke up. "We're not certain. We're in the process of reviewing the security footage to see if we can figure out who took the photograph."

The photograph. The one of him and Piper in the library last night. Clearly taken from the vantage point of the balcony right outside the second-story room. A part of the mansion that had been strictly off-limits to guests the night before.

"Our concern is that it was someone at the party, which will make figuring out who it was next to impossible. Unless we can find footage, and so far the tape we've scrubbed just shows a shadowy figure. We can't even tell if it's a man or woman."

Perfect. Frustration bubbled through Stone's body, making him restless. Pushing past Gray, he began to pace the length of the room, pulling at his hair. The pinch of pain helped to focus him on the problem.

"It's not that bad, man," Gray murmured as he stalked past.

On the surface, his friend wasn't wrong. But he wasn't right either. The photograph, snapped at the moment he'd picked Piper up off the floor after she'd collapsed, was clearly intimate. Something about the expression on Piper's face had sent heat storming through his body.

It wasn't simply the photograph that had him pacing. The headline accompanying it hit much too close to home.

Enemies to Lovers: Convicted Murderer and Victim's Stepsister

That headline was everything. Everything that he'd wanted for so long and everything he couldn't have.

He and Piper weren't lovers. Would never be lovers.

This was a truth he'd come to terms with a long time ago.

Now the entire city could see. Would whisper to each other about what a terrible person he was. Not that they hadn't already been doing that, but this time, Piper's name would get dragged through the mud along with his own. Everyone would pass judgment, not only on him, but on Piper. With saddened eyes and disappointed tones, they'd comment on how the well-respected psychologist should know better than to get entangled with the ex-con.

Whoever had taken the photograph had timed the moment perfectly to go along with the sensational innuendo. It looked like he was about to devour her, which couldn't have been farther from the truth.

In that exact moment anyway.

"Are you sure it wasn't her?"

Stone whipped his head around to glare at the man standing two paces behind Mitchell. "What did you say?"

Apparently, the man was either stupid or had a

death wish because he clearly ignored the warning Stone had just issued.

"You heard me. Could she have staged this whole thing?"

Gray's hand landed on his arm and squeezed. "To what purpose?" his friend asked.

"Maybe she's trying to get a little payback for her stepbrother? Making you pay just a little more in the media. Or maybe she's sold the story for money."

Stone laughed. "Piper hardly needs money."

"Are you certain? Correct me if I'm wrong, but her stepfather is the one with the money, right? Not her. She lives on his estate."

Stone's blood began to rush through his veins, an audible swish he could hear in his own ears.

"She's a psychologist with her own practice."

"That actually doesn't make much money considering the lifestyle she's used to living. She takes on quite a few pro bono cases."

Yep, that sounded exactly like Piper. "Let me guess, most of them are assault victims?"

The other guy's eyebrows shot up. "How did you know? She volunteers with several victim advocacy groups."

"I assure you, she doesn't need money."

"Her bank balance might suggest otherwise." The guy just wouldn't give up.

Stone was about to argue the point more, but Gray stepped between them, blocking his view. Giving him a hard look, his friend murmured, "You haven't seen her in ten years, man. How can you be so certain? People change."

And wasn't he the perfect example of just how true that statement could be. Could Piper have sold the photograph and story to the tabloids? She'd followed him. Knew where he'd be. Could she have staged the emotional turmoil he'd seen in her eyes?

His gut told him no, but was that simply wishful thinking? His time inside had taught him not to trust anyone...anyone except Gray and Finn.

Stalking across the room, Stone scooped his phone up off the floor. This time, he took the time to read every word in the article accompanying the picture. There was clear speculation about his and Piper's relationship when they were younger. But it wasn't like their friendship had been a secret. Most everyone knew they'd been close.

What did strike him was the speculation about why he'd cut off all contact with her while he was inside. A detail only a handful of people knew. First on that list being Piper.

Pounding reverberated through Piper's skull. It felt like someone had a jackhammer chipping away at her brain.

Obviously, she shouldn't have polished off the entire bottle of wine by herself after Carina left.

Prying one eye open, she looked up at the watery light spilling into her room from the windows. She'd forgotten to pull the curtains last night. This wasn't exactly how she'd planned to spend her Sunday.

Beside her, her cell phone buzzed against the nightstand. Glancing at the screen, Piper registered the word *Mom* flashing across the top. She wasn't in any frame of mind to deal with her mother just now. Rolling in the opposite direction, Piper's feet hit the floor at the same time the pounding began again.

Wait, that wasn't inside her head but at her front door.

Who the hell was at her door? It wasn't early, but was hardly a decent hour for visiting. Especially unannounced. And she definitely wasn't expecting anyone.

Grabbing her robe off the chaise, Piper slipped her arms into the silky sleeves. Her gaze caught on her reflection in the mirror as she passed her dresser. God, she looked like death. But she didn't have the will to care enough to do anything about it right now.

Not only would whoever was trying to break down her door most likely not allow her to take the few minutes she needed to run a brush through her hair, they didn't deserve the effort.

Stumbling downstairs to the front door, Piper yanked it open, words already flying from her tongue. "Stop pounding on the—"

The last person she expected to see glaring at her was Stone. Legs spread wide, like a pirate riding out a storm on the deck of his ship. His fist raised high, ready to strike against a wooden panel that was no longer in front of him. Thunder rolled across his dark expression.

Clearly, he wasn't any happier than she was.

"What the—"

He didn't even wait to be invited inside. Not that she had any intention of doing so. But he took away the satisfaction of refusing him entrance by brushing past her.

"Did you do it?"

Frowning, Piper shut her front door and stared at it for several seconds. She could ignore him, call her father's security team and have him escorted off the property. Something about that felt like a great idea.

Spinning on her heels, Piper faced him. One look at his expression had her thinking twice. She really didn't want any of the guys to get hurt trying to toss him. And it was clear Stone was a powder keg just waiting to blow.

Strangely enough, she had no concern for her own safety. She had no doubt he'd defend himself against anyone who came against him. But he wouldn't touch a hair on her head.

Even if she wanted him to.

Nope, that wasn't a thought she was going to consider.

The best way to handle Stone right now was to be the calm against his storm. But to do that she needed to figure out what had him so fired up.

"Did I do what?"

Stone's gaze narrowed, becoming glittering chips of hard amber. "Sell the photograph. Give someone details about our relationship."

"What relationship, Stone? We haven't been friends in a very long time."

Beneath the flush of anger, his skin paled. But that was the only evidence her words had hit a mark she honestly hadn't been aiming for.

Pulling a phone from his back pocket, Stone closed the distance between them and shoved it toward her face.

A photograph she'd never seen before filled the screen. A picture of the two of them. And she was wearing the dress from last night.

"Goddammit," she breathed out.

"You've either developed some very good acting skills or you didn't have anything to do with this."

Piper's gaze flew from the screen to Stone. She searched his face, looking for something other than the accusation ringing through his words. Anything.

Because right now, she was struggling against a rampant need to reach out and touch him. To run her fingers down the rough stubble covering his jaw. To pull him back to the bed she'd just rolled out of and leave the covers rumpled from something other than a restless night.

Stupid. Pointless. Maybe she wasn't quite sober after all.

Ripping her gaze away from him, Piper looked at the photograph again. Stone really thought she had something to do with the invasion of privacy she was staring at. "Go to hell."

Needing some space and a better understanding, she grabbed Stone's phone and paced away. Her finger stabbed at the smooth surface, scrolling and scanning as the words in the accompanying article flew by.

It was short, filled with innuendo and very little fact.

Piper spun on her heel to face him again when she was a safe distance away. "I'm assuming since you're at my door, y'all don't have any idea who's responsible for this?"

A muscle at the edge of Stone's jaw ticked. "No." He ground out the word between clenched teeth. "The security team is scrubbing surveillance footage as we speak. There was someone out on the balcony around the time we were in the library, but they're in shadow. We can't even tell if it's a man or a woman. But it looks like they knew exactly where the cameras were."

"Beautiful. You're saying it could have been anyone? Staff? Guest?"

"I have a friend who's trying another tactic. We're hoping to work backward from the photograph to figure out where it originated and maybe who sold it to the media outlet that sent it viral."

"You can do that?"

The corner of his mouth tipped up in a mocking half smile. It was a bastard version of the beautiful smile he used to spread around liberally, but there was something about it that had her belly taking a dive to her toes.

"I can't, but we know people."

"You know people? As in you know people who

don't have a problem breaking the law?" Was that what he was saying?

Stone shrugged, his massive shoulders straining against the cotton of his shirt. Piper swallowed, trying very hard not to notice...and failing miserably.

"They're not breaking the law. Exactly."

Piper's mouth twisted into a wry grimace. "Well, isn't that a relief. Are you *trying* to get thrown back in jail?"

His wide, gorgeous mouth twisted into a cocky grin. "I'm not the one skirting the gray areas of the law."

She wanted to shake her head. To wipe that coolly confident expression right off his face. To knock some sense into his thick skull. None of which would do much good, so she settled for saying, "Cold comfort."

This time the knowing grin he flashed her sent a storm of energy crackling across her skin. Yep, he needed to leave. Her defenses—and brain—were clearly still drunk on the wine from last night.

"Well, thanks for the wake-up call. Sorry I can't help you more, but it's time for you to go." Crossing the room, Piper opened the front door, squinting against the glare of sunlight as it stabbed into her eyes.

Stone stood stock-still for several seconds. His gaze raked over her, cataloging her entire body and leaving her restless and edgy. Her hair was a mess. She looked like hell. Not to mention her head pounded. Pride had her fighting back the urge to fix herself. Nope, she wasn't going to do it.

It didn't matter what Stone saw or thought. He would not intimidate her. She wasn't about to let that brooding gaze or his oozing irritation get to her.

It took everything inside Piper to bite her tongue and not fill the charged silence growing between them. But that's what he wanted, which was exactly why she wouldn't.

Slowly, Stone crossed the space. And, no, she didn't notice the way his body moved or the bunch and pull of his massive thighs straining against faded denim. Nope, not at all.

Pausing beside her, Stone reached for her. His fingers grasped a strand of hair that had fallen from the knot she'd pulled on top of her head. A shiver rolled down her spine as he followed the line to where it curled against her collarbone.

Goose bumps erupted across her skin the moment he touched her. But he didn't stop there. The warm weight of his hand followed the line of her shoulder and arm. His fingers brushed the back of her hand and for a second she thought he was going to tangle their fingers together.

Until she realized he was just reaching for the phone she still had grasped in her hand.

Leaning forward, his warm breath brushed across her skin as he murmured, "I need this back."

Piper immediately dropped it. If he hadn't already been poised to catch the phone it would have fallen straight to the floor.

She didn't care.

The connection between them needed to go away.

She'd felt the bond the day she'd met Stone when she was six. It deepened as they grew. Morphing, at least for her, when she hit fifteen. For so long, Stone had been her world. Her person. Until he wasn't. And she'd thought going ten years without contact would have killed the attachment, but apparently for her it wasn't enough.

And now Piper didn't know what to do with it. And that unsettled her more than she wanted to admit.

A knowing grin twisted Stone's lips and glittered at her from those golden, polished stone eyes. God, she wanted to smack him.

Stone used the edge of the phone in his hand to give her a little salute. "I'll let you know what we find."

"Don't bother. I don't care."

"Maybe not, but I do."

Goddammit. Fine, she did care. She just didn't want to admit it to him. And she definitely didn't want him worrying about her or taking care of her anymore.

"I'm fine, Stone. Go, live your life. Enjoy your freedom. Let me live mine."

In that moment, Piper wanted exactly that. For him, but also for her. She wanted to be free, as well. Unfortunately, something told her, wishing wouldn't make it so, for either of them.

* * *

Stone's fist slammed into supple leather. The jar of it reverberated up his arm, a comforting and familiar sensation. Beneath the punch, he could feel the shift of sand inside the weighted bag. His shoulders and arms ached with exertion. Sweat dripped down his face and into his eyes. He welcomed the sting.

It not only reminded him he was alive, but it took his mind off the picture of Piper, fresh from bed and heavy eyed, that kept playing over and over through his brain.

Because his mind was an antagonistic bastard hell-bent on leaving him with a permanent hard-on and the taunt that he couldn't do anything about it.

"Man, you might have enough energy to go twenty more rounds, but I don't." Gray's voice was muffled by the bag sitting between them. His body was braced against the swing of it, holding it in place as Stone swung again.

"A couple more," he panted out, not ready to let his body rest.

"I don't care how often you punch this bag, it isn't going to solve your problem."

"Oh, yeah? And what would that be?"

"That you can't make her do what you want her to."

"And what do I want her to do?"

Abandoning the bag, Gray dropped into the old metal folding chair he'd sat in the corner. Snagging a bottle of water, he downed half of it in a few heavy gulps before deciding to answer. "You'd prefer she be locked in a tower with no windows or doors."

"You've been watching too many animated movies, man. Maybe you should try something a little more hard-core."

"Funny. I notice you didn't suggest I was wrong, just attacked my choice of entertainment."

"No, seriously, try some porn. It might help you find your balls so you can punch that bag like a man."

Gray picked up the nearest thing to hand, which happened to be a sweat-soaked towel, and whipped it across the room at him. "Hurling insults won't make what I'm saying any less accurate. You can't make her do what you want, which pisses you off. She's not the little girl who followed you around with adoring puppy-dog eyes."

"She never did that."

Gray leveled a *bullshit* stare at him.

"Fine. There might have been a little hero worship when she was a little girl."

"Take it from me, there's still hero worship. She was watching you the other night."

That had Stone pausing midsip on his own bottle of water. "What?"

"At the party. I noticed her."

Stone's fist tightened around the plastic, hard enough that a spurt of water shot up and over.

"Stand down. Not that way. I mean, sure, she's absolutely gorgeous."

"Get to the point, asshole."

"I was lurking on the outskirts of the party. It's not like I knew anyone there so that's where I belonged. But she was there with me, a part of the group, but not really. It was obvious she did know quite a few people attending because they kept stopping her to speak. She was polite, but disengaged. And I wondered why she'd come since she clearly didn't want to be there."

Gray kicked back in the chair, lounging in a way that was completely relaxed. Something he couldn't remember ever thinking about Gray. People saw him as intense and intimidating, which Stone admitted he absolutely could be. Out of their group, Finn was the fun-loving fuckup that everyone loved because he was mischievous and always made you laugh. Gray's brain never stopped. He was always thinking, calculating and adjusting. He observed, which was apparently what he'd been doing the other night.

"Then I realized she was there because she was watching you. But she was also keeping her distance, which bothered me."

Not surprising considering the environment they'd both recently come from. There, you had to be observant and vigilant or risk getting stabbed in the back when you least expected it—often from someone you counted as an ally.

"At first, I wondered if she was pissed. Or had a vendetta. Then I realized, the way she looked at you…oh, she's plenty angry with you, but there's more. And something tells me there always has been."

Stone shook his head. He really didn't need Gray's words ringing through his brain right now. Not with everything all jumbled up after his visit to Piper's place this morning.

"It doesn't matter. I'm staying away from her. She has no reason to see me. I'll do what I can to shut down the media attention and we'll both move on with our lives."

Gray scoffed, the sound scraped against Stone's last nerve. "Good luck with that, man."

Five

Piper juggled the trays of mochas she'd stopped to pick up. The strap of her bag slid to the edge of her shoulder, threatening to fall right off and upend the careful balance.

The way her morning was going, that would just be the cherry on top.

She hadn't slept well last night, which meant she'd overslept and was running late. Something she absolutely hated. And she probably shouldn't have taken the time to stop and get a shot of caffeine, but it was the only chance she had to get her morning back on track. Without it…she'd be useless in her first session.

Something she hated even more than being late.

Feeling the need for some armor after the last

couple days, she'd dressed carefully and pulled out a pair of spiked Louboutin heels to match the power suit she'd chosen. And after about twenty minutes in them, she remembered why they'd been on the back shelf. They pinched like a son of a bitch, even if they were damn pretty.

Thank God she kept a pair of emergency heels in her office. She just had to make it there.

Rise and Grind was only a block away from her office, which meant it was a staple for everyone she worked with. Once she hit her desk, she was going to take five minutes to meditate and get her day back on track before seeing her first patient.

A sound peeled out from the depths of the bag that was hanging on by a dangerous thread. Whoever was on the phone was just going to have to wait until she could unload everything.

Turning the corner, it took Piper about five strides to register the melee halfway down the block. And then another few beats to realize the knot of chaos was standing right in front of her office.

Or it had been before the twenty or so people surged toward her like a tsunami, with just as much destruction in their intent.

Piper froze. She blinked, her brain already sluggish and unable to process what was happening. Voices bombarded her as the group closed in.

"Ms. Blackburn, how does your stepfather feel about you dating his son's murderer?"

"Can you shed some light on what happened between Anderson and Blaine?"

"How is Mr. Stone adjusting to being released from prison?"

"Doesn't it bother you to be sleeping with a murderer?"

Piper stared at them, her eyes wide, their words rushing over her in crushing waves.

Someone jostled her. Grabbed her arm to gain her attention. The trays of coffee tottered before going over. Dark liquid arced around her. People yelped and jumped back.

While she hated losing the caffeine she desperately needed, it cleared a path forward. Piper rushed through the hole like a professional running back, leaving the cups behind her, rolling across the pavement.

With a death grip on the strap of her bag, she barreled up the steps and crashed through the front door. Slamming it behind her, Piper sagged.

Elizabeth, a divorced single mom in her late thirties and her office manager, came racing into the front entrance. Her pale green eyes were filled with kindness and concern. But her body was relaxed. She was one of the most capable women Piper had ever met. She could count on one hand the number of times she'd seen Elizabeth truly upset, and all of those involved her son and daughter. She was unflappable, which was a real benefit for Piper's clients.

"I'm sorry," Elizabeth said.

"Why?"

"I tried to call and warn you. Anna had a meltdown about a class project this morning so I was running late."

Piper laughed, the sound a little thready, but still there. "Apparently, we're all having a stellar morning."

A soft smile curled Elizabeth's lips. "I'm thinking you might win this competition, Piper. You have coffee all over your suit."

Looking down, Piper realized Lizzy was right. She hadn't even felt the heat or wetness hitting her. "Fracking hell."

"Yep, that about sums it up."

Behind her, someone turned the knob and tried to open the door. It moved about half an inch before colliding with her shoulder and shutting again. Piper barely had time to react before it moved again.

"What the…"

She recognized Mrs. Collins's voice. Her first appointment every Monday morning.

Jumping out of the way, Piper yanked the door open. Mrs. Collins, a petite woman in her sixties, stood on the front stoop. Her bleached blond curls, perfectly coiffed in a mane two inches around her head, quivered. The pearls she always wore at her throat were cockeyed and the blazer she'd put on this morning was hanging off one shoulder.

Piper understood exactly how she felt.

Behind her, the group of vultures surged forward, using the opportunity to hurl more questions at Piper.

Grasping Mrs. Collins by the arm, Piper yanked her inside and slammed the door again.

The three women stood there, staring at each other. Mrs. Collins blinked owlishly. Her mouth opened and shut. Opened again, but no sound came out. Shaking her head, she tottered over to a nearby chair and dropped into the soft leather.

Great. This wasn't going to help the other woman's recovery after being assaulted.

Anger slowly welled inside Piper. This wasn't okay.

Kneeling in front of Mrs. Collins, she grasped the other woman's hands and looked her in the eye. "Are you okay?"

She cocked her head and truly considered the answer before squeezing Piper's hand. "I'm a little shaken up, but I'm fine." Her grip tightened and something sharp flitted across her expression. "Are you okay?"

Piper's lips twisted into a self-deprecating smile. "Yes." Even if she wasn't—and she wasn't entirely certain whether she was yet—she wouldn't burden a patient with the truth.

Mrs. Collins apparently wasn't having any of that. She cocked a single eyebrow, her gaze flitting down Piper's suit and purposely lingering on the coffee stains that were starting to dry. "You know, it doesn't do you or anyone around you any good if you're not honest about how you're feeling."

This time the laugh Piper let out was absolutely

genuine. "I'm not sure how I feel about having my own words used against me."

The other woman shrugged. "Sometimes we need to hear the tough things from someone else."

"Very true. I'm shaken up. And I'm pissed. But I'll be okay."

"Now that sounds more like the truth."

"I'm so sorry you had to deal with this." Glancing up at Elizabeth, Piper said, "We need to reschedule all the appointments for this morning until I can get this taken care of. Please tell anyone we move that they're welcome to call me directly if there's anything they need to discuss before we can get them back in."

Nodding her head, Lizzy left to have it taken care of.

"Mrs. Collins, I'm sorry, but I think it's best if we reschedule your appointment, too. I'll ask Anthony to take you out the back door and escort you to your car."

With a smile, she reached up and tapped Piper on the cheek. "That would be lovely. He's such a sweet boy. Reminds me of my Douglas."

After getting Mrs. Collins squared away, Piper crossed the front room. Her office was a beautiful town house in a section of town that had been turned from residential to commercial several years ago. It was the perfect setting for her practice. Cozy and not clinical. Welcoming and comfortable. She'd carefully designed the interior.

The front room was a cross between a parlor

and a reception area. There was a sofa and a couple chairs, all oversize and leather. In the winter there was always a fire burning in the fireplace. Her office was located in the back. She'd knocked down a wall to combine two rooms to give her plenty of space.

Right now she wasn't worried about the decor though. Crossing the room, Piper pulled back the heavy linen drape covering the large picture window and frowned at the group of people milling just off her property on the sidewalk by the street.

Had the group of them grown? Probably.

Behind her, she heard the office door open and close. Lizzy strode across the room to stand at the window with her. She made a sound in the back of her throat, a cross between disapproval and irritation.

"Right there with you," Piper responded. It was about all she could say.

Reaching beyond her, Lizzy pulled the curtain closed, blocking out the chaos on the street.

"You want to talk about it?"

"Not really."

Lizzy nodded, but apparently wasn't willing to take Piper at her word. "He's handsome as hell."

"What?"

"Anderson Stone. I'm just saying, he's handsome as hell."

Piper frowned. "I guess I've never thought about it."

Lizzy's eyebrows rose, silently calling her on the lie. "Please."

Piper shrugged. "We were just friends. Before. And now we're nothing." The words sounded off even to her own ears.

"Uh-huh. That picture didn't look like nothing."

And that was the problem, wasn't it? The reason a dozen reporters were camped out in front of her place of business. The moment captured in that photograph was innocent, but beneath the layers of civility there'd been something more.

There'd always been something more.

And now everyone could see it, even her amazing but boring office manager.

But the bigger problem was that she didn't want there to be nothing. She wanted so much more, even if she shouldn't. Even if wanting wouldn't get her anywhere.

Rather than respond to Lizzy, Piper pulled back the curtain again. At least this was a problem she could solve.

Fishing her phone out of the bag she'd dropped by the door on her sprint inside, Piper called her stepfather. She'd never needed his security team's help before, but she wasn't too proud to ask for it now.

Especially when her patients were being affected. This had to stop.

Stone stared out the large window of his father's office. Below him, he watched as several trucks loaded with steel pulled away from the building. Behind him, he could hear the mundane sounds of an office at work even through the closed door. And if he took the time to walk across to the next building, he'd hear the clings and clangs of a working mill. He'd see the people who spent their lives supporting the legacy his family had built.

And he felt guilty.

Because he really didn't want to be there.

Nothing about Anderson Steel had ever excited him. But ten years ago, he'd been absolutely ready to devote his life to the company. Because it was what was expected. Because it was his legacy. Because he never wanted to disappoint his parents, who had taken the business and grown it into an international powerhouse.

It was amazing how losing your freedom could change your perspective. He'd taken the time to get the education he needed in order to be successful at stepping into his parents' shoes. And, yet, he was less inclined to actually do it now.

He'd already given up ten years of his life. Years he didn't regret. But he wasn't ready to commit the rest to doing something he didn't love.

The problem was, he had no idea what he did want to do, which made saying no very selfish.

The door behind him opened, the office noise getting louder, but Stone didn't bother turning. He already knew it was his dad. Mostly because the other man was issuing instructions to the staff that constantly followed behind him. "Make sure I get the report from Tokyo before the end of the day. I won't accept any more excuses."

He'd heard that tone from his dad more than a

few times in his life, gruff and with a tinge of disappointment sharpening the edge. It was never a comfortable experience and for a brief moment Stone felt sorry for whoever was late on the report. But that didn't last when the door closed with a quick snick, muting everything beyond the office again.

He was not looking forward to this conversation.

His father didn't bother saying anything as he crossed the room and came to stand next to Stone. Together, they watched the scurry of activity below them in silence.

Finally, his dad said, "Stop, son."

Slowly, Stone's head swiveled. "What?"

A brief smile flitted across his father's face. "I can hear your brain going like a freight train from here, son. I didn't ask you to come in today to force you to do anything you don't want to do, so stop worrying."

"I don't understand."

Shaking his head, his dad walked to the big chair behind his desk, spun it out and dropped into it. "You're my son, Stone. And I've always known that taking over Anderson Steel wasn't high on your wish list of career options."

"What?" Was he a broken record today? "Then why the hell did you pressure me to pursue business at Harvard?"

His dad shrugged. "When you were younger you didn't seem to have another path that you preferred so I pushed you into business hoping you'd find whatever sparked your passion…and if you didn't then you'd be prepared to take up the reins here."

"And why did you offer me a job when I got out?"

"Because I wanted to make sure you knew that you had not only my full support, but the support of the company and board. Do you think they would have allowed me to bring you on if they thought you were going to be a liability?"

No, now that he thought about it, he didn't. God, he was so stupid for not realizing that immediately. He had an MBA for God's sake. He should have been thinking through the implications of the offer, not drawn into a mental tailspin trying to decide how to respond. Yet another failure he could add to the tally.

Maybe at the core of everything, he'd been so worried about giving his father an answer because he didn't feel worthy to be part of Anderson. To help carry on his great-grandfather's legacy.

He'd gotten his MBA in prison for God's sake. Not exactly the path most high-level CEOs would take. Not only didn't he want to be here, but he didn't deserve to be here.

"You don't need to have an answer today. Or even next month. The offer is on the table and I have no intention of retracting it. But I want you to take the time to get comfortable and figure out what you really want. Your mother and I have only ever hoped for your happiness, Stone."

Stone stared at his dad, unable to stop himself from comparing his own family to Gray's, who had disowned him, even in spite of his repeated protests that he hadn't been guilty of the embezzlement he'd been convicted of.

And here Stone was, absolutely guilty of manslaughter and his parents were accepting him just as he was. Even though he'd never shared with them the extenuating circumstances surrounding Blaine's death. They'd simply accepted he was the man he'd always professed to be and that he wouldn't do something like that without justification.

"I love you, Dad."

Warmth flashed through his dad's deep brown eyes. "I love you, too, son."

Suddenly, overwhelmed and exhausted, Stone collapsed into the chair across from his father's desk. Tugging a hand through his hair, he closed his eyes and just took a few seconds to breathe. The weight he hadn't realized he was shouldering eased a little.

The comfortable silence that had settled over the room was broken by the sudden buzzing of a cell phone. His dad leaned forward to check the screen resting on his desk. Grabbing it up, he answered, "Morgan, how are you doing?"

For some reason, Stone's body went tight.

His father and Piper's stepfather were more than neighbors. They'd been friends for years and had a monthly poker game with several of Charleston's business elite. That friendship had continued through Blaine's death and Stone's incarceration. So there was nothing unusual about Morgan McMillan's phone call.

Except the expression on his dad's face.

"No, our PR team has been fielding all requests and declining them. Stone's been purposely staying close to home so they wouldn't have a target. I'm so sorry that's left Piper exposed."

Stone shot out of his chair, the heavy wooden legs scraping loudly across the marble floor. "What?"

His dad held up a finger in Stone's direction. "Yes, I'll have our team issue a warning to the media and I think it's a good idea to give her some extra security. I'll send someone from our team right away."

Stone's hands ached. Looking down, he realized he was gripping the edge of his father's desk, his knuckles bright white from the effort. Letting go, he shook out his hands.

"No, I insist, Morgan. This is our responsibility. We knew there might be issues so my team is prepared... I'm just sorry Piper is taking the brunt of things right now. But we'll keep her safe."

His father dropped his cell to the desktop and sagged back into his chair. "Goddammit."

"What's going on?"

"Apparently, without another target handy, the paparazzi has decided to camp out in front of Piper's office. Obviously, that's a problem considering what she does. She can't have media recording her patients coming and going from her office. It's a major privacy violation."

Picking up his cell again, his dad started making phone calls. Stone paused long enough to hear him tell the head of security at Anderson Steel to send a team to Piper's office, which was great.

But Stone wasn't about to wait.

Six

"I'm so sorry about this," Piper said, listening to the voice at the other end of the phone and staring out the windows of her office. "Yes, of course we can schedule an extra appointment for next week if you feel it's necessary. But, Margaret, I don't know that you need it. You're making such great progress. I have faith in your ability to handle the next few days on your own. And you know I'm only a phone call away if you need me."

Ending the call, Piper stood from her desk to get a better look at the street a story below. Yep, they were still camped out on her front stoop.

Flipping her wrist over, she looked at her watch. It had been three hours since she'd called her stepfather. Some officers had shown up to clear the street, but once they were gone the reporters had returned. She was expecting a couple of his security team to show up shortly.

And after spending the last couple hours speaking with the patients she'd had to reschedule, she was feeling a little restless and a lot impatient.

There were two things that would scatter the vultures sitting outside. One, if a tastier story came along to distract them. Or, two, they got at least a small piece of something to satisfy their appetite.

She'd never been the kind of person to sit and wait for someone else's misfortune to save her and she wasn't about to start today.

Arms crossed, Piper stared down at the knot of people milling just off her lawn. One of the women was familiar. Not only because she was a local media personality, but also because she'd personally approached Piper several weeks ago when Stone's release was announced. The woman had clearly been fishing then, so she'd been easy to dismiss.

But maybe Piper could use their previous interaction to her advantage. Crossing to her desk, Piper dug out the business card she'd carelessly tossed into a drawer and flipped it over several times without actually looking at the information embossed on the glossy surface.

Thoughts whirled through her brain. Images she tried not to think about merged with her encounter with Stone from the other night. Past and present melded together in a jumble that left her feeling off-kilter. Damn, she wasn't sure this was the right move, but she didn't have another idea right now.

Picking up her cell phone, she dialed and quickly made an appointment. She was setting it down again when a commotion in the hallway startled her.

A door slammed.

"You can't just barge—" Lizzy's raised voice bounced down the hall.

The door to her office burst open, slamming into the opposite wall before rebounding to smack against Stone's tall frame standing in the middle of the doorway.

Behind him, Elizabeth peered around his large shoulders. "I'm so sorry, Piper. I tried to stop him."

"It's fine." It wasn't, but it was hardly *Elizabeth's* fault Stone's rough edges were apparently out to play again today. "I've finished calling all the patients. Please let everyone know that if they don't have anything else pressing, they can take the rest of the day off. Hopefully, things will have settled down by tomorrow."

"I wouldn't count on it," Stone sniped under his breath.

Piper chose to ignore him. "Thank you for your help today and I'll be in touch later to let everyone know about tomorrow."

"Are you sure there's nothing else I can do for you," Elizabeth asked. With a quirked eyebrow, she gave Stone a quick once-over before throwing Piper a pointed glance.

They'd worked together long enough, and developed enough of a silent language that Piper knew exactly what Lizzy was asking.

Was she sure she wanted to be left alone with Stone?

If she was smart, the answer would be no. But that was hardly for the reason Elizabeth might expect.

"Nope, I'm good. I promise."

Lizzy shrugged. "If you're sure."

The minute she closed the door, shutting Piper and Stone into the office, she wanted to take it back. But she wouldn't. Couldn't.

Sweeping a hand at the two armchairs she often used for sessions, Piper silently asked him to have a seat. Maybe she just needed to treat this—and him—like any other person she was attempting to help.

Stone frowned, but dropped into the chair before saying "I'm sorry" in a hard voice that belied the words.

"No, you're not."

Tipping his head to the side, he studied her for several seconds before finally agreeing. "You're right. I'm not."

"You've never lied to me before, no reason to start now."

That was the one thing she could say with absolute certainty about their relationship. They'd told each other the truth, no matter what. Although, obviously there were things then—and now—she'd simply chosen not to address. But she wasn't willing to view that as lying by omission.

Although, for the first time ever she began to wonder what *he* might have kept to himself…

"What are you doing here, Stone?"

"Morgan called my dad about the reporters outside your office."

"And you thought the best way to keep the gossip from blowing up even more was to show up here?" He'd never struck her as unintelligent, but that had to be the most asinine thing she'd ever heard.

Which meant she did not understand the incredulous expression on his face. "I came in the back door."

"Oh, because they couldn't possibly be watching my alley?"

"I was careful, Piper. I'm pretty used to watching my back and being aware of my surroundings."

Goddammit. "Whenever you say stuff like that it just inflates my guilt."

"That's not my intention."

"I'm aware, which only makes it worse."

"That's not why I'm here."

"Obviously. So how are you going to save me this time?" The minute the words were out of her mouth, Piper wanted to take them back. They sounded petty and ungrateful, which couldn't be any farther from the truth.

"I have no idea."

It took a minute for Piper to realize what Stone had said. "Excuse me?"

"You heard me."

"Yeah, but I was pretty sure my brain had processed something incorrectly. Because why would you come all the way down here, risk being seen and making things worse, all without an actual plan?"

Piper wasn't sure which emotion was stronger, incredulity or anger. "Seriously, Stone. Did your time in prison zap all of your intelligence, because that's probably the stupidest thing I've ever heard you say."

Something hard flashed through Stone's eyes, but it was gone practically before she could register the emotion. Sagging back into the chair, he rubbed his hands across his face for several seconds before finally erupting into laughter.

The sound of it, deep and rich, rolled through her. It made her skin tighten and places she didn't want to think about right now tingle.

"Yeah, probably not the smartest move I've ever made."

Which begged the question, why had he done it? But for some reason, Piper didn't really want to ask. Possibly because she wasn't ready to hear the answer.

Leaning forward, Stone stared at her. The expression on his face was…so serious. So direct. Piper felt his gaze straight at the center of her gut. Restless energy, uncomfortable and unwanted, began to crackle just beneath the surface of her skin.

Hell.

Needing to move, Piper stood up and walked a couple paces. "Well, thanks for stopping by?"

But she didn't get far. Stone lunged after her, grasping her upper arm and holding her in place.

"Piper."

That was it. Just her name. But she heard so much more behind that single word. Frustration, yearning, denial.

Or maybe she was just projecting.

Warmth from his fingers seeped through the flimsy fabric of her shirt. How could his simple touch make her burn? She didn't want this. Didn't want him.

And that was such a lie.

"What?" Jerking her arm, Piper tried to get some relief from the dangerous sensation. But he wouldn't let her go. His hold on her tightened as he rounded the chair, invading her personal space.

Stone had been closer than this more times than she could count. As little kids they'd slept in the same bed. Many summer nights they'd found a patch of grass at the back of her stepfather's property, her head in his lap as they'd had contests about naming the constellations. Even as teenagers, before things had changed, they were constantly touching each other. Innocent exchanges.

Nothing about right now felt innocent. At least not to her.

Which was why she needed to get Stone out of there before she did or said something embarrassing.

"What are you going to do?" he finally asked.

The heat of him radiated across her side, where he held her. Piper purposely didn't turn to him, struggling not to give in to this craving for him that just wouldn't go away.

"Piper?"

"What?" she croaked out.

"What are you going to do?"

"About what?"

"The reporters camped outside your front door."

Oh, yeah, that. "Well, I'm hoping a couple men from my father's security team will be here shortly to clear them out of the way. Again."

"That's only a temporary solution."

"True. Which is why I've contacted a local reporter and agreed to an exclusive interview with her."

"You did what?"

There was something about the dangerous quiet in Stone's voice that had her gaze whipping to his. Anger sparked through his eyes, reminding her of the tiger's-eye stone she'd bought on a field trip to the natural history museum as a child. She'd chosen it then because it reminded her of his eyes, all gold and brown swirled together in a pattern that mesmerized her.

"We're meeting in—" Piper's gaze flicked to the clock mounted on the wall behind Stone's head "—a couple hours."

"Why would you do that?"

"Because it's the best way to get their attention off of me. One of my patients had to walk through that crowd on her way in this morning. Most of my clients are recovering from traumatic experiences, Stone. Do you know how devastating that encounter was for her? She was a shaking mess when she got inside. I had to reschedule the rest of my clients today."

"I never thought you'd become the kind of woman to care about losing billing hours."

Disappointment and sadness filled Piper. She wanted to be angry, but couldn't find it in herself. This, right now, was cold, clear evidence that Stone no longer knew her. And it hurt.

"You might not know me anymore, Stone. But you know enough to understand my motives have absolutely nothing to do with money."

Something hard flashed through Stone's gaze, but it was immediately replaced by regret. "I'm sorry, you're right. I know your motive is to help people."

His words helped, but they didn't completely take away the sting…or the regret for what they'd lost.

"But that doesn't make an exclusive a good idea, Piper. Talking to the press is going to stir the pot and make you more of a target, not less."

Piper shrugged. "I disagree. I'll give them what they think they want and they'll go away."

"You know better. You've been around the media long enough to understand that's not how things work. Ignore them for a few days and a bigger story will come along to take the heat off."

She laughed, the sound cracked and brittle. "Please. You weren't here, Stone. You missed the media storm that followed Blaine's death and your confession. Everyone has been waiting ten years for the full story."

"Well, they can wait a hundred more because they're not getting it."

"No, they're not. But ignoring the media completely isn't going to make them go away. Oh, they might get distracted for a little while, but they'll keep coming back. Hell, it's been ten years and they haven't lost interest. But we can use this to our advantage. Give them a little taste so they go away for good."

It was Stone's turn to laugh, the sound scraping down her spine like nails across a chalkboard. "If there's one thing I learned inside, Piper, it's that you don't mess with someone who has more power than you do. Not until you're damn sure you can beat them. Talking to anyone right now would be a mistake. You don't have anything valuable to offer…and you suck at lying. You're more likely to slip up and make yourself a bigger target than you already are."

"Forgive me for not being versed in deception, but I'm just going to have to risk it."

Using his hold on her arm, Stone applied pressure until she turned to face him. Slowly, he shifted closer. Air stalled in Piper's chest. Her lungs hitched, trying to pull in oxygen even though nothing seemed to be working right.

She needed space.

Taking a step back, she tried to find some distance. But Stone had no intention of letting her have it. Instead, he followed her. One step. Two. Five, until her back collided with something solid.

His voice was low, rough. His jaw flexed, teeth grinding together. "Don't, Piper. Don't talk to them."

He was upset. Piper could clearly see that. But it didn't matter. "Unfortunately for you, there's nothing you can do to stop me. I'm a big girl, Stone. Perfectly capable of taking care of myself and making decisions about my own life. I've been doing just fine without you for a while now."

Something sharp pinched in the center of her chest. She wasn't sure which made breathing more difficult, the way Stone loomed over her or the pain of the truth she'd just given voice to. Dammit.

Stone growled beneath his breath. He shifted, the solid wall of his chest brushing against her and drawing a soft gasp from her parted lips.

Whispering an expletive, his hold on her shifted. His arm snaked around her body, lifting her up onto her toes. Before she could register what he was doing, his mouth hovered above hers.

She leaned toward him, and everything changed.

He had no idea what he was doing. But that didn't matter. The millisecond the warmth of her mouth touched his nothing else mattered.

Like it ever could.

The flat of his palm slapped against the door beside her head. Piper's leg wrapped high across his hip. Her fingers gripped his shoulders, pulling her body tighter against him.

He'd never wanted to devour anything or anyone as much as he wanted Piper.

Her lips parted beneath his, giving him the access he desperately craved. The taste of her, sweet with a dark hint of coffee, flashed through him. And he wanted more.

One taste would never be enough.

That thought was clear, even as everything else in the world faded to nothing. Stone didn't care where they were. Who was close. Or what was going on around them. All that mattered was Piper and the way she was melting against him.

His fingers twisted in her hair. Stone tilted her head so he could get more of her. Their tongues tangled together in a dance that was years late. Her nails curled into his skin, digging in and leaving stinging half-moons. But her tiny, breathy pants made the bite insignificant.

He needed more of her.

Reaching between them, Stone began to pop the buttons on her blouse. One, two, three. The backs of his fingers brushed against her silky, soft skin driving the need inside him higher.

Pulling back, Stone wanted to see her. He'd been fantasizing about this moment for so long. He didn't want to miss a single second of it.

Piper's head dropped back against the wall. She watched him, her gaze pulsing with the same heat burning him from the inside out.

But instead of letting him finish the buttons, her hand curled around his, stopping him.

The tip of her pink tongue swept across her parted lips, plump and swollen from the force of their kiss. Moisture glistened. He leaned forward to swipe his own tongue across her mouth, to taste her once more.

But her softly whispered words stopped him. "Let me go."

Immediately, Stone dropped his hands and took several steps away.

Conflicting needs churned inside him. No part of him would consider pushing when she'd been clear that she didn't want his touch. But the pink flush of passion across her skin and the glitter of need in her eyes…he felt the same echo throbbing deep inside.

"I'm sorry."

"You seem to be saying that a lot, Stone," she murmured.

"I shouldn't have done that." He felt the need to say the words, even though they felt wrong. Everything inside him was screaming that he should have kissed her. Should have done it a hell of a long time ago.

Touching her, tasting her, wanting her was right. The most right thing he'd ever done.

But it wasn't.

Piper deserved so much more than he could ever give her.

Turning away from her, Stone dropped his forehead against the door he'd had Piper pinned against. "It's been a long time since I've touched a woman, Piper."

"Gee, how flattering. I was your friend for years and you never once expressed any interest in me as a woman. But give you ten celibate years behind bars and I'm good enough to want."

"That's not what I meant." Turning, Stone pressed his back against the hard surface of the door. Several paces away, Piper stood, arms wrapped around her body and bravado stamped all over the gorgeous features of her face.

God, she was beautiful.

Pushing away from the door, Stone stalked closer. "Let's get a couple things straight."

He had to admire the way she stood her ground, although she couldn't quite hide the desire to move. Not with the way her shoulders swayed away from him before she squared them up again.

Her chin notched up and her bright blue eyes glinted with fire. Amazing. A grin twitched at the corners of his mouth, but Stone was smart enough not to let it free.

"First, I've never needed to use sex to get anything I want and I have no intention of starting now. And, yes, that means exactly what you think it does, considering where I've been the last ten years."

Piper's eyebrows slammed down into a tight frown. Her mouth opened for a second and he waited to see what kind of remark she might make to that confession. But she snapped her lips shut without saying anything.

"Second, I've wanted you for a long damn time, Piper. But I *needed* you as my best friend and wasn't willing to lose you over a little lust. We were both too damn young and not ready for anything permanent."

Reaching out, Stone let his fingers slide across the soft skin of her cheek, down the curve of her neck and across the silky surface of her shoulder. She shivered, goose bumps erupting across her skin. Her eyes dilated, deep pools of black pushing against the gorgeous ring of blue that would forever remind him of a perfect summer sky.

"Luckily, neither of us is young anymore," he growled before turning on his heel and walking away.

It was either that or push everything off her desk and take her right there.

And Piper deserved a hell of a lot better than that.

A hell of a lot better than him.

Seven

Piper's head was still spinning. What had he meant they weren't young anymore?

Even several hours later, her skin still tingled where Stone had touched her. The echo of it reverberated through her body. Very inconvenient considering who was sitting across the desk from her right now.

She could dissect the minute details of the experience and try to decipher what Stone wanted from her later. Although, she wasn't likely to come to a different conclusion now than she had earlier.

Which was: she had no clue.

"You grew up together?" Madelyn Black shifted in her seat.

The woman was professional, gorgeous and had

a reputation for being the kind of reporter who was fair and ethical. Piper wasn't completely stupid and had checked before agreeing to speak with her.

"With Blaine or Stone?" Piper asked, stalling for time to get her head back in the game.

The hint of a smile tipped up Madelyn's plum-colored lips. The dark color suited her skin tone and perfectly matched the tight skirt and blazer she was wearing. Something told Piper that wasn't accidental. The woman clearly knew how to put pieces together to create a picture. "Both."

"Yes. I was six when my mother married Blaine's father."

"She was a teacher, right?"

"Yes. At the private school Blaine attended."

"But you didn't go there?"

"Not until later."

Madelyn made a humming noise beneath her breath and jotted a note onto the pad of paper in front of her.

"I met Stone soon after moving onto the estate. Our families have always been close."

"All accounts suggest you and Stone were insepa-rable as children."

"I suppose that's true. Until he graduated high school and left for college, we saw each other daily."

"That must have been difficult."

"What?"

"Him leaving you behind."

Piper shrugged. "That's life. It was difficult, but

also not unexpected. I wanted him to do the things he wanted and live the life he envisioned."

"Instead he ended up in jail for murdering your stepbrother."

Madelyn paused, probably in the hopes Piper would make some response. Fill the silence. She could wait a very long time.

"Do you know what the fight was about that night?"

"It was my graduation party. I was a little pre-occupied with my friends."

Another smile played at the corners of the other woman's lips. Piper expected Madelyn to press, to fling a series of rapid-fire questions at her, hoping to trip her up and get more information. Instead, she seemed to switch tactics.

"Tell me about the photograph."

Piper swallowed. Beneath the desk, she unfurled the fingers that had folded into cramped knots in her lap.

"A misunderstanding."

"It always is." This time Madelyn didn't bother to hold her reaction back, revealing the bright white smile that had won her hordes of local adoring fans and would catapult her onto the national news scene sooner rather than later.

This coup was going to help her achieve that goal. Which was part of the reason Piper had chosen her. Madelyn Black was hungry…and would hopefully accept the gift she'd been handed wrapped with glittery ribbon.

"Stone and I were…having a conversation."

"A passionate conversation."

"You could say that. I was angry with him."

"Are you still?"

Piper couldn't stop the short bark of laughter. "Occasionally." Piper shrugged. "I haven't seen or spoken to him in ten years. We had a couple things to hash out. The photograph was taken out of context. I realize it looks like we were about to kiss, but we weren't. We were both angry."

"Have you?"

Piper shook her head. "Have I what?"

"Kissed."

Her mouth opened and then shut. Her brain spun and her skin heated. Crap. She couldn't lie. As Stone had said, she was terrible at it and her expression was going to give her away.

"Yes."

"Interesting."

"Not particularly. We didn't kiss that night and there's nothing going on between Anderson Stone and myself. There never has been."

Madelyn shifted in her chair, settling against the straight back of it, and watched her for several seconds. "I'm not sure who you're lying to, me or yourself."

"I'm not lying to either of us, Ms. Black. I promised you an exclusive interview, but unfortunately, there's really no story here. At least none the public might be interested in. Both my family and Stone's family are trying to move past what happened. We're finding our way. Our families are close, although you can imagine what happened has put a strain on all of those ties."

"Oh, certainly. But not enough for you to boy-cott the welcome home party of the century for your stepbrother's murderer."

"Human relationships are complicated, Ms. Black. People and situations can rarely be viewed through a black-and-white lens."

"I noticed your parents didn't attend the party."

"Of course not."

"But it's well-known your stepfather and Stone's father are still friends. They play golf, attend a weekly poker game and are members at the same country club."

"They're business colleagues, Ms. Black. And adults. They have the ability to recognize punishing each other for the actions of their offspring makes no sense."

"Interesting."

"What?"

Madelyn waved her hand. "Oh, nothing. Except I'm not sure what Stone's father would have to pun-ish Blaine's for."

Piper swallowed. Her fists locked again in her lap. "A simplified expression."

"I'm sure."

Piper's chest was tight. Beneath the jacket she'd layered over the pale blue silk shell, her skin was clammy. Had someone turned on the heat?

A soft knock sounded on the door before Lizzy

stuck her head around the edge. She'd decided to stay after Piper had told her about the interview. "I'm sorry to interrupt, but you asked me to remind you about your next appointment."

Thank God and Lizzy for the little white lie.

"Thanks, Elizabeth. I'll be right there."

Madelyn stood, holding out her hand across the desk. Piper gripped it, accepting the show of professionalism even as she fought the urge to jerk away. "I appreciate your time, Ms. Blackburn. I'll be in touch if I have any follow-up questions."

"Certainly." Although, Piper had no intention of being available when or if the other woman called. She'd said as much as she was going to.

And something told her Madelyn was smart enough to realize that.

"I'll show you out," Elizabeth offered.

The minute the door shut behind the women, Piper collapsed back into her chair. The casters rattled beneath her. How could a twenty-minute interview leave her feeling like she'd run a seven-hour marathon?

She'd hoped to end the interview feeling better. Like she'd solved a problem. Instead, there was a huge part of her worried Stone might have been right.

Had she just made everything worse?

God, she hoped not. Because there was no part of her that wanted to hear *I told you so* from him.

Even the simplest thought of him had her skin burning and her lips tingling.

Dropping her head against the back of her chair, Piper closed her eyes, which didn't help when memories of their shared kiss flooded her. She needed to deal with her reaction to what had happened with Stone.

Why now? Why had he kissed her now?

For years she'd fantasized about the feel and taste of him. The heat and feather-soft touch of his fingers on her skin. But she'd given up that fantasy a long time ago.

Even before Blaine.

Because at no time had Stone given her the impression he was interested in her that way. She was his best friend. Practically his little sister. The first time she'd caught him kissing another girl had felt like a dagger through her chest. The day Colleen Heath had bragged she'd had sex with him, Piper fought against ripping the other girl's self-righteous smirk right off her face.

He wanted other girls, but not her. Never her. She'd simply assumed he wasn't attracted to her.

But their kiss suggested that might not be the case.

At least not anymore.

The question was…what was she going to do with the information? And did it really make any difference?

"I'm thinking about letting a leprechaun rent my place so I can move to Antarctica."

Stone shook his head, turning to look at Gray. "What?"

"Just making sure you were still with me, man."

"I'm with you."

"I'm pretty sure you didn't hear a word I've said in the last five minutes. Until I threw in the leprechaun at least."

Stone was completely lost. Because Gray wasn't wrong. His brain had been a scrambled mess from the minute his mouth had touched Piper's.

But he wasn't stupid enough to admit that, not even to Gray. Maybe especially not to Gray. "I heard you."

"Uh-huh. What did I say?"

Stone grimaced. "You were telling me how ineffective our cyber contact is."

"No, my guy's the best of the best."

"I don't see how you can claim that since he hasn't produced any results."

"Not his fault. These companies have layers upon layers of protection in place to shield their sources. Shell corporations, untraceable offshore accounts. Hell, he's pretty sure they used a dummy drop of cash. Who uses cash anymore?" Gray shrugged and shook his head. "They've gone out of their way to protect the source of this juicy tidbit. Probably in the hopes they can get more."

Stone couldn't suppress the growl that rumbled through the back of his throat.

"Piper isn't a juicy tidbit."

Laughing, Gray clapped a hand against Stone's

shoulder. "You sure about that? Even if the media didn't think so, you obviously do."

Stone stared at his friend and seriously contemplated decking him. Two things stopped him. One, Gray wasn't necessarily wrong, even if Stone might want him to be. And two, the man was a fricking powerhouse with his fists. He might look relaxed as hell in a power suit, but the man had moves like Ali and had dominated the underground fighting circuit they'd had going on the inside.

A knowing smirk played at the corners of Gray's mouth. *Bastard.*

"My guy isn't giving up. It's just taking him a little longer than anticipated. We're not his only project."

Stone didn't like that at all. "That's a problem. What'll it take to make this his highest priority?"

Dropping into a large leather armchair, Gray steepled his fingers and studied him for several seconds. "I've gotta be honest, I'm not sure there's a benefit to throwing more money at this now."

"What are you talking about? Of course there is. I need this story to die so I can get on with living my life."

Gray rubbed a hand over his face. "You've never given me the details about what happened."

Unlike Gray, who'd eventually shared everything with him and Finn, and Finn, who'd been all too happy to boast about his exploits even when no one was asking, Stone had never shared. Not even with his closest friends.

"You never asked." And as far as he was concerned, that had made their bond even stronger.

"I didn't need to know. I recognized a man with integrity and trusted that whatever happened, you had good reasons for what you did."

A pregnant silence filled the space between them. Stone's teeth ground together, tightening his jaw against the words that inexplicably wanted to come out. It would be easy—and natural—to share everything with Gray. For ten years they'd been as close as possible given they were both locked behind bars. On more than one occasion Stone had literally trusted Gray with his life. Instinct and history told him he could trust his friend with the whole truth now. Something he'd always known.

But it wasn't his story to tell.

And the more people who knew what had happened the more likely that something would slip.

"Are you asking me now?" he finally asked.

"I don't really have to, man. I know you well enough to fill in some of the blanks. What I can't figure out is exactly what her stepbrother did…but I can guess."

Goddammit. Gray was too smart for his own good. Stone racked his brain for some response that wasn't the truth, but wasn't a lie.

Gray beat him to it.

"It doesn't particularly matter. Finding out where the photograph came from is potentially a moot point—so giving our hacker more money isn't going to solve anything. The article from your girl's interview is going to hit the press in about—" Gray flipped his wrist over to look at the heavy platinum watch "—two hours."

"What?"

"That's actually what I came by to tell you. My guy might not have uncovered our source, but he did discover the Associated Press is about to run with a major story based on the interview she granted to that hungry reporter with the sleek hair and perfect tits."

What the hell was wrong with her? "I warned her not to give the interview."

"Hmm, something tells me she decided to ignore you. Shocking."

"Fuck off. How bad is the damage?"

"Bad enough. Instead of diffusing the conjecture, it sounds like she added fuel to the fire. The article is full of speculation that you and she were in the middle of a private affair that her stepbrother walked in on and went ballistic over. Adding another juicy bone to the already meaty pile is an anonymous source providing details that Piper and Blaine weren't close. And that he was actually pretty terrible to her."

Stone wanted to throw something. Break something. A dark pit churned in his belly. How many times was he going to have to save her from herself before she realized he knew what the hell he was talking about?

"The shit's about to hit the fan."

Stone's mouth twisted in a wry grimace. "No.

Really? The question is what can we do about it? I assume your guy's already tried to kill the story?"

"No point. He could throw a kink into things and delay the release, but the information is out there and they'll just find another outlet. Too many to police them all. You could attempt a lawsuit to prevent the release, but you and I both know you don't have a legal leg to stand on. The best that does is gain you some time."

"It also makes the story look even more damning."

"Exactly."

He and Piper were both about to become media magnets. Bigger than they already were. Piper thought the frenzy outside her office was bad before…it was about to get ten times worse. Thanks to Anderson Steel's security team he had some insulation. And while Morgan could offer her help, he assumed Piper would be her stubborn self and refuse.

The woman was infuriating.

And that was before his brain had short-circuited from the taste of her. Right now, even though he was irate enough to chew through nails, mixed with that anger was a ribbon of white-hot need he couldn't seem to ignore.

Or rationalize his way out of anymore.

"So, what are you suggesting?"

"How likely is it that she'd agree to disappear for a while?"

Stone laughed, the sound brittle and harsh. "Piper

doesn't understand the phrase *lay low*. She's stubborn as hell and doesn't like to be told what to do."

"And, yet, you keep trying. Maybe you should attempt another tactic?"

Gray had a point. Piper hadn't exactly been open to his suggestion last time. In fact, she'd run right out and done what he told her she shouldn't. Maybe this time he wouldn't suggest.

He wouldn't give her a choice.

Stone needed her out of the spotlight. Far away from the media so she couldn't make things any worse. The best way to do that was to isolate her. For a little while.

An idea formed in Stone's head. He flipped it over a few times, poking holes at it and testing for weaknesses so he could be certain.

"I've seen that light in your eyes before, man, and it usually doesn't lead to anything good. What are you thinking?"

"Just that you're right."

"Why doesn't that give me the warm and fuzzies like it's supposed to? Last time you had that calculated, determined expression on your face I ended up in the infirmary with a gaping hole in my side and you were in solitary for a week."

"Yeah, but it was worth it, right?"

Gray tilted his head and studied Stone for several seconds before slowly nodding. "Yes, to see the expression on G-man's face was totally worth it. But I'm not certain we'd feel that way if it had turned out differently."

"But it didn't. Trust me."

"Oh, I do. That doesn't mean I don't think whatever you're planning is going to include a ton of trouble."

"You like trouble."

"Lucky for you."

Eight

Exhaustion pulled at Piper. Her entire body felt like she'd gone a couple rounds with an MMA fighter. And her brain was just...done. For the second day she'd had to cancel all of her appointments. And that pissed her off. Her patients hadn't asked for this mess. Although, none of them had complained. But that didn't stop the guilt. They had enough trouble dealing with the drama in their own lives. They didn't need to be dealing with hers, as well.

She'd held it together all day, but the minute she'd walked through her own front door all she'd wanted was to collapse, cry and potentially drown her sorrows in an entire bottle of wine.

While she'd counsel any patient that coping

mechanisms were fine, an entire bottle of wine was probably excessive. So she'd compromised.

After a single glass and a long soak in a hot bath, she was feeling a bit more centered. Still drained, but less like she was about to collapse under the weight of everything.

Snuggled up in her most comfortable, and oldest, pajamas, she'd decided to indulge a little more with a good romantic comedy on TV, a quick salad for dinner and the chocolate fudge brownie she'd been saving. Chocolate fixed everything. At least for a few minutes.

She was just about to click Play when her front door reverberated beneath the solid pound of a palm against the heavy surface. Piper practically jumped out of her skin. One of the benefits of living in the cottage was that not many people just showed up at her door.

Unfortunately, that also meant no one had ever seen the benefit of installing a peephole. The only way she could discover who was on the other side was to yell or open the door. She was about to yell when Stone saved her the trouble.

"Open up, Piper. I know you're home."

Standing a few feet away, Piper crossed her arms and glared at the door. "No. Go away. I'm not in the mood for another lecture."

Or kiss.

She wasn't strong enough to handle that right now. And, to be honest, one of the reasons she refused to open the door was because she didn't trust herself to keep her hands to herself if he crossed her doorstep. Her defenses were already too low.

Piper braced for an argument that she had no intention of losing. This was her home, dammit, and she decided who came inside and who didn't.

But a few seconds ticked by. And then a few more. A minute with no response from Stone. She took a step closer, straining to hear anything, but there was no sound. Finally, with a shrug she turned back to her spread in front of the TV.

Maybe for once he was listening.

Her butt had just hit the cushions of her sofa when the front door swung open. Piper yelped, upending the plate her brownie sat on.

Stone's wide frame filled the doorway. Light from her porch backlit him, giving the illusion of a halo surrounding his dark head. *Please.* There was nothing saintly about the man.

"What the hell!" Piper growled, glaring down at the brownie, fudge icing side down, at her feet. "I've been saving that."

Without a single sign of remorse, Stone swept inside. He scooped the brownie up off the floor, deposited it back on the plate and said, "Good as new."

"Hardly. Leave."

"Sure."

Piper's belly flipped. Yeah, right. Nothing with Stone was ever that easy.

Wrapping an arm around her waist, Stone turned and headed for the door, sweeping her along with him. Instinctively, she rocked back onto her heels, digging in and trying to stop his momentum. "Let me go."

"Absolutely, once we're somewhere safe."

"What do you mean, safe?" Piper spun out of his grasp. "Stone, stop."

"That interview you granted is about to make life even more difficult than it already was. You need to disappear for a little while."

"And you thought the best way to do that was sweep in and just take me?"

Stone shrugged. "Pretty much."

"It didn't occur to you to discuss this with me? Ask my opinion?"

"Sure, but the last time I asked you not to do something you did it anyway. And made things worse. I figured this time I'd just jump straight to what needed to happen."

A frustrated sound rolled through her chest. "You're infuriating. You know that, right?"

"So I've heard. That doesn't change anything, Piper. When that article hits the streets you won't have any peace."

"My practice."

"Is shut until this calms down. What you've dealt with the last couple days is going to look like a company picnic compared to the hoard of vultures about to descend. This story is hitting the Associated Press. It's going viral."

Piper threw her hands into the air. "So where am I supposed to go? If it's viral there's no place to hide. No place to escape the scrutiny."

Stone smiled. Any other time the wolfish show of teeth might have given her pause, but right now... the man looked like he was about to go up against his worst enemy and had an ace up his sleeve to guarantee a win. He looked excited, which scared the hell out of her.

"Luckily, I have the perfect spot. The family happens to own a private island in the Caribbean. And a jet to get us there."

"I'm not going to the Caribbean right now, Stone. Not leaving everyone else to deal with this mess."

"Trust me, we're doing everyone a favor by disappearing. Just for a few days. Let the initial frenzy die down. Give us a chance to come up with a media strategy."

Piper opened her mouth to protest. She didn't want to form a media strategy, dammit. Especially when Stone wouldn't stop formulating long enough to listen to what she actually wanted.

"One we can both agree on." Taking a step closer, Stone held his hands up in front of him. "I promise, Piper. I'm trying to help here. Please, let me."

The scent of him tortured her. He was so close she could have reached out, pulled him in and brought his mouth to hers. Her lips tingled at the mere suggestion. Her body hummed, energy pulsing just beneath her skin.

How was it she could be so frustrated with him and still need him so badly she could barely think straight?

And he wanted her to go to some private island with him?

Could she resist this driving need if they were alone and she couldn't escape?

But almost stronger than the need to touch and taste him was the desire to let him help. She wanted to go back to a time in her life when she could lean into his warmth, feel the weight of his arms wrapped around her shoulders and know he could solve anything for her.

But that wasn't fair to him. And it wasn't fair to her either. She was strong enough to solve her own problems.

How many times had she looked a patient in the eyes and told them that asking for help wasn't admitting weakness though? It took great strength to admit you couldn't handle something on your own and trust someone else to share the burden.

Above anyone else, she trusted Stone to protect her and keep her safe, something she apparently needed right now.

Groaning, Piper closed her eyes. "Fine."

She just needed to find a way to accept his help without giving in to temptation and doing something stupid. Should be easy, right?

Being ignored was really starting to piss him off. Maybe Stone was stupid for expecting that Piper's reluctant agreement to his plan would mean her cooperation with everything else. And it wasn't like she'd thrown a temper tantrum or anything. She'd simply chosen to pretend he was invisible.

For their six-hour flight she'd waited to choose a seat until he'd sat down...and then picked the chair farthest away from him. And proceeded to open a tablet and not bother to look up again until the wheels touched down on the tarmac.

Transferring from the airport to the docks where they picked up the boat for the ride out to Isle D'Acier had been much the same. If she could avoid direct communication, she had. When that wasn't possible, single-syllable words had been the extent of her response.

And he'd had it. Stone's patience was stretched thin and his irritation was about to win out over his temper.

Stone had requested the normal staff be given several days off once the estate had been stocked with the supplies he'd asked for. Considering the viral nature of the story that had hit the streets while they were somewhere high above the Caribbean, he didn't see the need in providing temptation for any of the staff. They'd been vetted and most had been under the corporation's employ for years.

But money was always a motivating factor that was often difficult to ignore. Stone wasn't in the mood to take any chances. Privacy was a better option right now.

And that meant there wouldn't be an audience for the clash that had been brewing for the last several hours.

Stone held the front door to the ten-thousand-square-foot estate open and gestured Piper through. She skirted around him, making damn sure her body didn't come close enough to touch him.

That didn't stop the buzz of awareness from crackling across his skin as if she had. Stone's fist tightened around the edge of the door, the corners biting into his flesh and helping to ground him.

A few feet inside, Piper dropped the bag she'd slung across her shoulder onto the sideboard in the entrance. Spinning on her heel, she braced her feet wide and tipped her head to the side. "Point me in the direction of my room, please."

Her body language said she was perfectly aware of the energy brewing between them. Her words suggested she planned to ignore it and pretend it didn't exist. Her strategy of choice tonight.

The restless energy beneath his skin said that ship had sailed hours ago.

Stalking forward, Stone let the front door slam shut behind him, plunging the entrance into a gloomy darkness. To her credit, Piper didn't bother to move a muscle as he invaded her personal space.

"Stop acting like the six-year-old brat you never actually were, Piper. You're better than that."

A harsh sound scraped through her throat. "Apparently not. I'm not in the mood right now, Stone. Tell me where my room is. From the looks of this place, it's big enough we should be able to avoid each other for the next several days."

Yeah, that wasn't going to work for him.

"Are we just going to ignore what happened?"

To her credit, she didn't attempt to pretend not to understand what he was talking about. "Nothing happened. You said yourself that you've been without a woman for ten years. That's a long time. Especially for someone with your appetites."

"What do you know about my appetites?"

She shrugged. "Let's just say your reputation was well-known, even to me. Honestly, it was embarrassing when I was younger. Do you know how many girls approached me looking for information on how to bag the legendary Anderson Stone?"

The ripe bitterness in her voice surprised him. Rocking back on his heels, he asked, "Why didn't you ever say something?"

"What the hell was I supposed to say, Stone? That it bothered me whenever someone shared some tidbit of gossip about your latest sexual conquest? Would that have changed anything? Made you stop? I don't think so."

Stone reached for her. He wasn't sure why or what purpose he hoped to achieve. No, that wasn't true. He wanted to soothe away the echo of the pain he'd had no idea he was indirectly inflicting all those years ago.

But she flinched away, rejecting what he was offering.

Balling his fist, Stone let it drop back to his side. "I'm sorry."

A tiny huff of humor pushed through her open lips. "For what exactly?"

"Hurting you."

"Sure. It's easy to say that now. The problem is you don't realize you're still doing it. I'm not sure you know how to stop. So, where's my room?"

The irritation he'd been nursing for hours, building into a roiling ball of righteous indignation, crumbled away to nothing leaving him stupefied and uncertain. Both things he didn't particularly relish.

"You take the master. It's down the second hall to the right at the very end."

Piper spun on her heel and took several steps before stopping suddenly. Without turning, she asked, "Where are you staying?"

"The room next door."

Her head dropped. The long line of her light brown hair brushed across her back. The light caught highlights of gold, making it glint and drawing him unwittingly closer. Stone wanted to bury his hands deep in the strands, to tip her head back and claim her mouth. To touch her and tame her. Soothe her and promise he wouldn't hurt her again—intentionally or unintentionally.

But he stopped himself. Because right now, that's not what she wanted from him.

"I'll move to another room."

"No. I will."

Twisting her head, she looked at him over her shoulder. She hadn't taken the time to put on makeup before they'd left and for the first time in years he could see the freckles that sprinkled across her pert little nose.

He loved those freckles. Before, they'd been a sign that beneath the layer of her seriousness, she was still a little girl. When she'd gotten older, he'd needed that reminder to keep his own needs in check.

Now…he simply wanted to kiss every damn one so he could never forget the taste of her skin.

"Will you?"

"Yes."

Finally, she nodded and walked away.

True to his word, she hadn't heard or seen Stone all night. Wherever he'd settled, it hadn't been close to her.

And, no, she wasn't irritated that he'd finally listened to her and done what she'd asked. Not at all. It didn't bother her that she'd had to roam the huge house alone in order to find the kitchen and make herself something to eat.

Whoever had stocked the estate had outdone themselves. It wasn't like she'd spent hours in the kitchen slinging pots and pans—although maybe that would have been a good thing. At least, it would have kept her busy and her mind from wandering.

To Stone.

She'd had an assortment of prepared meals to choose from. So she'd taken the most amazing spiced chicken with some sort of salad back to her room and had eaten it standing in the doorway of her private patio, staring at moonlight streaming across the sand and water.

And, nope, she didn't think about how amazing it would have felt skinny-dipping in that warm water.

With Stone.

Not once.

Her "not-thinking" hadn't helped her restless night. She'd slept poorly and was cranky this morning. Coffee was definitely on the agenda. And since she was stuck on this private prison for the next several days, she'd decided to enjoy herself.

She'd spent the plane ride over trying to take care of all her patients. She'd contacted an old friend who was going to see those who couldn't afford to miss sessions. He'd also agreed to be on call for the others in case something came up. For the first time since she'd opened the doors to her practice, she had no responsibilities.

And it felt entirely weird.

Which was also probably contributing to her restlessness and irritation. Piper knew herself well enough to recognize that she didn't operate well without a task to accomplish. So she was going to concentrate on figuring out how to relax. This was going to be good for her.

Grabbing a banana from a bowl on the large kitchen island and a huge mug of coffee, Piper slipped back to her room. Staring at the suitcase she'd packed, she cursed Stone once more. He'd barely given her twenty minutes to throw things together and since it wasn't like she prepared for a Caribbean vacation often, she'd completely forgotten to grab a swimsuit.

Just for kicks, Piper walked into the large dressing room attached to the master suite and simply stood there staring. An entire array of clothes filled the space.

At first Piper thought they were Stone's mother's, but after a few seconds she realized all of them had tags hanging from the garments. They were new.

She was going to kill him if he'd asked the staff to stock this closet for her. It was too damn much.

But that didn't mean she was above taking advantage of the one thing she actually needed. Moving to a built-in, she opened several drawers, certain she'd eventually find what she was looking for. And wasn't disappointed when one drawer revealed a handful of swimsuit choices in every color and cut.

Piper grabbed several, shed her clothes and started to try them on. She shouldn't have been surprised when they were all in her size and fit perfectly.

The first was a one-piece that might have been considered modest if the hips hadn't been cut high enough to reveal half the swell of her butt cheeks and the front hadn't been cut in a V so low that the tip touched her belly button. There was no way she was wearing that anywhere. The next choice was a two-piece, a little more conservative, but the bright stripes just didn't fit her.

The last one though…

Piper stared at herself in the full-length mirror for several moments wondering if she had the courage to wear it out. No, that wasn't quite right. She had the courage…she just wasn't sure the move would be smart.

The suit was a deep sapphire blue that somehow managed to make her eyes pop even though she hadn't bothered to put on any makeup. The top might have been conservative except for the straps that crisscrossed over her chest in a way that drew attention to the deep cleavage it managed to create. The bottoms covered her ass, but rode low enough on her hips to give the impression they might just slip off at any moment and leave her naked.

She should try something else. No doubt about it.

But she didn't want to.

This suit made her feel sexy, something she hadn't realized was missing in her life until right that moment.

Screw it, she was going to wear it.

Snatching up a beach towel from the stack left in the bathroom, Piper pushed open the sliding glass door and walked onto the beach. The sand, still cool from the night, gave way beneath her feet.

All around her, wild vegetation ran rampant, Mother Nature trying to reclaim what Stone's family had attempted to tame. At least for a while.

Piper stood at the edge of the water. She was completely alone. It was an unusual sensation. Even in her cottage, she was cognizant of the fact that she wasn't ever truly alone. Her parents were never far away. And the surveillance cameras on the property meant someone was always aware of her comings and goings. Even at her office, her staff was there, anticipating her needs and providing their help.

But here…she was.

Tipping her head back, Piper closed her eyes and just breathed. So much had been happening in the last few days that she hadn't taken the time to simply be.

Cool water lapped at her feet, swirling around her ankles before being pulled back out again. The soft sand shifted beneath her, allowing her feet to sink deeper and deeper until she was afraid she might be stuck.

Maybe that wouldn't be such a terrible thing.

Peace washed over her with every lap of a wave and Piper soaked up every second.

She had no idea how long she stood there. But she did know the exact moment she was no longer alone.

The weight of his gaze on her was tangible. Energy raced up her spine and sped through her veins. No one except Stone had ever made her feel this way, restless and awakened and yearning all at once.

It was seriously inconvenient and annoying.

"Do you want me to leave?"

Did she?

"No." The answer was simple, the reason behind it not so much. "It's your house, you can stand on the beach if you want."

But that didn't mean she had to. Turning, she started back toward the house, but Stone shifted, putting himself straight in her path.

"Stay."

He didn't touch her. In fact, he remained several feet away from her. Hands shoved into the pockets of his loose athletic shorts, his posture was far from intimidating.

But it didn't matter.

Stone's gaze quickly skimmed down her body, leaving her breathless and aching. Never in her life had she felt more naked. Which was laughable since she'd thrown on a flimsy, flowing cover-up that hid everything.

"That's not a good idea," she finally answered.

"Why?"

"Because I'm still angry with you."

"Maybe, but when has that stopped you? It's not like I haven't managed to piss you off multiple times before."

"Somehow, I don't think this equates to the time you put blue Silly String in my hair."

Suddenly, his warm eyes began to twinkle. Laughter brightened his face, even if the sound didn't actually come out of his mouth. She'd do anything to make him laugh. The thought was a shot through her brain before it could even register.

There was such a difference between the man standing before her and the one she'd seen in the library the night of the party. Or the one who'd coerced her into coming here yesterday. Piper was fully aware of the rough edge prison had given Stone, but never more than in that moment. The difference made her heart ache.

Because it shouldn't be.

"You were so mad." He took several steps forward, closing the gap between them. A half smile on his lips, he picked up a strand of her hair and ran it through his fingers. Piper fought back the shiver that tripped down her spine.

"I'd just spent the better part of an hour curling my hair so it would be perfect when Jeremy Rivers came over to work on our group project. Something you knew."

"I didn't know you'd gone all girl on me. You'd never given a damn before then."

"Bull. You knew."

The smile faded. His gaze skipped from his fingers tangled in her hair to snag her eyes. The punch of it made her stomach flip. Piper swallowed, her throat working hard against the sudden dryness.

"You're right. I was jealous as hell. You'd never taken ten minutes to do your hair for me."

If he only knew. But making that confession probably wouldn't be smart. So Piper had no idea why her mouth opened and whispered words fell out.

"You're wrong."

Nine

Stone stood there, staring at her. Sun streamed across her body making the pale white linen of the dress she'd thrown on practically transparent.

His head throbbed. His half-hard dick did, too. Every cell in his body was pounding for him to take. To scoop her up, lay her down on the soft sand and explore every inch of her luscious body.

Her rosy lips were parted and her eyes were slightly glassy as she stared up at him. Her soft words reverberated through him, a confession ten years too late.

Yet another tragedy in the long line of them that littered his life.

Gritting his teeth, Stone forced his hand open.

The silky threads of her hair brushed across his skin as he stepped away and let her go.

Nodding toward the water, he said, "Why don't you get settled for the day? I'll grab us something for breakfast and bring it out."

He didn't wait to see her response before slipping back into the house. He needed the breather before he did something stupid.

Something else Piper would never forgive him for.

Pulling things from the fridge, Stone made a platter of cheese, meat, fruit and added some crusty bread. Frowning at the pitcher of fresh orange juice, he debated the intelligence of making mimosas and decided champagne couldn't hurt.

He definitely needed something to take the edge off and it was too damn early for Scotch.

Pushing open the floor-to-ceiling windows that stretched across the back of the house so that the warm breeze could flow inside, he loaded his arms down and brought everything onto the large stone patio.

There was a lap pool made of dark, slick stone, but he rarely used it. Why would anyone prefer chlorine-laden water when the Caribbean was steps away? A hand-carved gazebo covered the fourteen-foot rough-hewn table that stretched across the patio.

The space was made for entertaining, but probably not in the way most people would expect. His parents didn't host lavish parties, at least not here.

This space was for family and friends. It was comfortable and easy. Welcoming.

He had so many good memories here and hadn't realized how much he'd missed it until right now.

Studiously keeping his gaze from straying to the beach, he spread everything out before yelling for Piper. The scent of salt and something sweet followed her when she settled into the chair next to him. Already, her skin had a pale pink tinge to it.

"Be sure to put on sunscreen. You're not used to the sun and it'll hit you quickly if you're not careful."

Shrugging, Piper popped a grape into her open mouth. "Thanks for the warning."

They finished breakfast with little conversation. It wasn't exactly uncomfortable, but it wasn't entirely pleasant either. Like a riptide, an undercurrent neither could see pulled at them.

Stone had no idea what to say to Piper, which was an unusual situation. One that would have to end because eventually they'd need to discuss what was happening back home. At the moment Gray was monitoring everything and providing updates. He'd had their hacker tap into the surveillance feed at Piper's place and her practice so they could keep an eye on things.

Reporters had shown up at her office again today, but once they realized she wasn't coming in they'd scattered. No doubt they were all scouring the city trying to figure out where she'd holed up. Little did they know she'd slipped right out from under their noses.

And since there wasn't a pressing reason to bring

it up, Stone decided to leave the subject alone for now. Piper needed some time. And he wasn't ready to deal with her temper again just yet.

After breakfast they silently worked together to clean up. Piper insisted on washing their dishes even though he told her someone—someone he trusted—would be by in the afternoon for a quick run-through and to bring them anything they needed. She disappeared back into her room for a few minutes before reemerging with a paperback in one hand and a bottle of sunscreen in the other.

Piper slipped back outside. Stone purposely waited for a while before following her down to the beach. By the time he arrived she was settled on one of the bamboo lounge chairs, a large floppy-brimmed hat covering her head and hiding most of her face.

Unfortunately, it did nothing to hide her body.

Her pale skin—and there was a lot of it to see since the bikini she was wearing barely contained enough material to be classified as clothing—glowed beneath the kiss of the clear Caribbean sun. One leg was bent, toes tucked beneath the rounded curve of her calf. Her nails were painted a deep, dark red that was surprising, but probably shouldn't have been.

When had she become a siren?

At some point, Stone had simply stopped moving so he could stare. His feet were anchored to the sand. His throat felt like he'd scooped up some of that sand and tried to swallow it. Not to mention his swim trunks were rendered obscene by the erection trying to rip through the fabric.

Realizing he was there, Piper dropped the paperback she'd been reading into her lap and craned her neck around. Stone quickly dropped the towel he'd been carrying so that it covered his predicament.

"You gonna skulk there all day or come enjoy the beautiful view?"

He was already enjoying the most beautiful view on the island. But he was smart enough to keep that thought to himself. For about three seconds, Stone contemplated settling into the chair farthest away from her, but decided while that might have made things easier, it wasn't where he wanted to be.

And he'd never been one to take the easy path anyway.

Throwing the towel at the foot of the chair, Stone settled beside her. She wasn't wrong, the view really was gorgeous. In the distance, Stone could see another island. It was owned by some oil tycoon he'd never had a reason to meet when he was younger. The house was on the other side of the property, which meant their view was of the untamed jungle as it climbed up and over the peaks of a small mountain. The island was lush and for some reason reminded him way too much of the woman sitting beside him.

Closing his eyes, Stone tried to settle. It was something he'd become very good at doing when he was behind bars. When someone had no control over things like when to eat, sleep and shower, one learned to control what one could. He'd become adept at controlling himself, his emotions and his reactions.

But today he couldn't convince his brain to switch gears. All he could see behind his eyelids was the vision of Piper's body. The need for her pulsed through him. It would be so easy to reach over, pick her up and settle her across his lap.

To take what he wanted.

Even though he didn't deserve it. Didn't deserve to touch and taste her. Not when doing so would taint her with everything bad inside him.

"How did you get inside my house?"

"What?" His brain was having trouble keeping up.

"Yesterday. How did you get inside my house?"

"I picked your lock."

Slowly, Piper turned to look at him. She tilted her head back so the brim of her hat lifted out of the way. "Excuse me?"

"You heard me."

"It took you less than ninety seconds to pick my lock."

"Yes."

"What the hell did you learn in prison, Stone?"

He laughed, the bitter sound scraping against his own ears. "Don't sound so scandalized, Doctor. I also managed to earn several degrees, including a masters."

"In addition to acquiring some nefarious skills."

Stone shrugged. "There's a lot of free time in ten years."

A bitter smile twisted her gorgeous lips. "And you don't like to be idle."

She knew him so well. "True. I might have been in a low-security prison, but it was still prison and several of the men had skills they were all too happy to show off."

"And share."

"Let's just say I'm a quick study and you never know when a skill is going to come in handy. Especially there."

"Promise you'll never use that skill on me again."

"Nope, not gonna happen."

"You realize that's a violation of privacy, right? No one should live with the expectation that a locked door is never actually locked."

Stone's gaze swept across her face. So earnest. But beneath the steady hold of her blue eyes he could see the echo of fear. And hated that it was there.

"I'd never hurt you, Piper."

"That's not why I want to lock you out, Stone."

He shouldn't ask the question. He knew it. And, yet, the word slipped out anyway. "Why?"

The pulse at the side of her throat pounded in a way that made him want to pull the skin into his mouth and suck. To leave a mark. One that every other man would see and understand.

"I don't trust myself. You make me feel things. You always have. Everything with you is bigger. More overwhelming. I don't always like who I am with you."

Her words punched him straight in the gut.

Mostly because she was the person who made him want to be the best man he could possibly be.

But she wasn't finished. Her confession continued. "I can't control it, Stone. This need for you. It's inconvenient and I don't trust myself not to do something we'll both regret."

"Rest assured, I can handle you, Piper."

"I know. That's what scares me most."

Piper couldn't believe the words coming out of her mouth. The confession she'd had no intention of making. The power she had no desire to hand him.

But she couldn't lie to him either. Although, that saying about the truth setting you free was a bunch of BS. She wasn't free. She was even more tangled up than before.

They sat in silence. Piper half expected to see lightning crackling across the horizon, the energy arcing between them was that thick. She could smell it, like burnt ozone mixed with the unique, spicy scent of him.

Her body felt heavy. Her limbs too weighted to pick up and leave.

No doubt, he felt it, too. Every muscle in his body was drawn tight with the same tension pulsing through her. The weight of his gaze settled on her, making her chest feel tight enough to crush her lungs.

Finally, he shifted. Stood. She half hoped he was going to come to her. To push them both to one side or the other of the razor's edge they'd been walking for days.

Piper held her breath. And let it out in a single gust when he backed away. "I'm going to go for a swim."

"Good. Yeah. A swim." God, she sounded dazed and completely out of it.

His mouth twisted into a half smile before he spun on his heel. Instead of heading for the ocean in front of them, he moved back toward the house and the pool.

Nope, she wasn't disappointed that she was going to miss the show of him coming out of the water half-naked, sunlight catching droplets as they clung to the tight abs he'd developed in the last ten years.

Education wasn't the only thing he'd picked up in prison.

Someone needed to knock her upside the head so maybe her own intelligence would resurface. Where was Lizzy when she needed a good lecture? Or Carina when she needed a glass of wine and girl time?

Flopping back in the chair, Piper screwed her eyes closed and whispered, "Get a grip," mostly because she knew that's what her friends would say if either of them were here.

Right. Rolling onto her belly, Piper reached behind her to pop the clasp on her bikini top and buried her face into the towel she'd rolled into a makeshift pillow.

A nap and some sunshine…that's what she needed.

* * *

"You little fool." The soft timbre of his voice rolled over her like a caress. Even if his words weren't exactly endearing, the brush of his fingers across her naked skin made up for it.

Heaven. Piper arched into his touch. The movement was instinctive, something she couldn't have stopped even if she'd wanted to.

And she didn't.

She wanted him. Wanted his hands on her. More than her next breath.

A fog hung over her brain. But not the scary midnight kind where monsters lurked. A soft morning haze. The kind that wrapped her in a blanket and shut out the rest of the world when what she really wanted was a few extra minutes in bed before the day had to begin. There was no reason to rush it away. Not when Stone was there with her.

Piper buried deeper into the soft bed, relishing the luxurious feel of wallowing.

Until something cold splatted onto her back, breaking the spell.

"What the hell," she yelped, jumping up and flipping over at the same time.

Sleep made her gaze bleary, the fog now disorienting. She batted blindly, connecting with something solid. The momentum of her flailing sent whatever it was tumbling to the ground with a deep thud.

Stone perched on the edge of her lounge chair, glaring down at her. "You fell asleep in the sun," he snapped. "You're already pink. Sunscreen." He pointed to the bottle lying in the sand beside them.

His eyes blazed at her, a mixture of anger and desire that he wasn't making any effort to hide. Her body reacted, coming alive. Everything inside her pulsed with awareness and longing. With a bone-deep need that was so acute it bordered on painful.

Piper licked her tongue across her lips. They were suddenly so dry and she needed relief. Any relief.

Stone's gaze raked down her body. Her nipples tightened. The pinch and tingle, the answering tug deep between her thighs, made her pull in a sharp breath. A breeze tickled across her naked skin and for the first time she realized her top was still lying on the chair beneath her.

Grabbing up the towel from a nearby chair, Stone handed it to her. "Cover up."

The order, almost as much as the rough edge to the words, had her hackles rising. Batting it away, the towel landed uselessly on the sand beside the sunscreen. "No."

Stone blinked. His jaw grinding together. "No?"

"You heard me."

"Piper, listen to me very carefully. I'm hanging on by a thread here. Put your damn top back on."

Her body burned. The heat from the midday sun was no match for the heat his nearness caused. Everything inside her wanted that thread to snap. She wanted the wild passion she could see him struggling to control.

She wanted to forget her own struggle to deny what she'd wanted for so long.

Staring at Stone, the pressure filling her chest popped. And every excuse she'd ever had for pretending she didn't want him disappeared.

Slipping her legs beneath her, Piper pushed up onto her knees. "No," she breathed. "I won't put it back on. What are you going to do about it?"

With a growl, Stone grasped her upper arms and hauled her against him. The hard press of his body made her dizzy. Or maybe that was the intoxicating scent of desire going to her head.

Slowly, he dragged a hand up her back to bury it in the hair at her nape. His palm cupped her head, angling her just where he wanted her. Holding her still. Making her wait.

She could have broken free of his hold, but she didn't want to. She was breathless with the need for him.

With a gentleness that contradicted the strength she could feel pulsing through his body, Stone bent to brush his lips across the curve of her cheek. A shiver rocked her as moist heat caressed her skin.

Her eyes closed. The better to relish the sensations he was creating. Her body sagged into his hold, unconsciously giving him everything. All of her.

His mouth found the tender shell of her ear, the heat of his breath slipping over her. His other hand began to draw light circles over her shoulder, down her spine and across the curve of her hip. It wasn't enough. She needed more. Needed the storm he was holding back.

She made a sound in the back of her throat. A mewl, a request, a demand.

His teeth sunk into her earlobe, drawing a gasp and making her entire body arch against him in surprise. But before she could react, he was soothing the shock away, the rough edge of his tongue laving against the tender spot.

And he finally answered her. "I'm going to give you exactly what you want."

Ten

He couldn't let her go. Not again. Not when she was so warm and willing in his arms. Not when she'd practically dared him to take what they both clearly wanted.

Apparently, he wasn't nearly as strong a man as he'd always hoped.

God, her skin was so soft. And the scent of her... it filled his head until it was all he could think about. All he could taste.

He'd walked out to tell her he'd made some sandwiches for lunch and found her sound asleep. She'd looked so peaceful. He hadn't been able to keep himself from walking closer, which was the moment he realized her skin was turning pink from the sun.

Applying sunscreen had seemed like the intelligent thing to do. Maybe he should have woken her up first, but he'd thought it would be easier, less temptation, if she was asleep.

He'd never been more wrong.

When she'd flipped over, her eyes still unfocused and heavy, her hair a tangled mess around her gorgeous face...he'd had to fight the urge to push her onto her back and kiss the hell out of her.

Then he'd realized she was naked from the waist up and every other need he'd ever had in his life disappeared to nothingness. Still, he'd tried to do the right thing.

But Piper, headstrong, beautiful, infuriating Piper, hadn't let him.

So he was finished fighting what he wanted.

Arm around her waist, Stone pulled her closer. Her skin, warmed from the sun, smelled like a mix of coconut and spice as he drew her in. His teeth found the tight line of tendon that ran down her throat. Latching on, he sucked, pulling the taste of her deep into his mouth.

God, she was intoxicating.

Her hands raced across his body, sending waves of need crashing through his system. He wanted more.

And apparently so did she. Her hands landed on his chest and shoved. "Oh, yeah? And what exactly do you think I want?"

Giving in to the momentum, Stone let his body fall backward onto the double chaise.

But he sure as hell wasn't going alone.

Using his hold on her, he pulled until Piper followed, sprawling across him. The impact of her had the breath inside his lungs whooshing out.

"Obviously, you want trouble. You've been spoiling for it since we left your place."

"No, I've been fuming since we left my place."

"Same thing."

A soft laugh rushed through her open lips and across his skin. "No. No, it isn't."

Tangling his fingers in her hair, Stone surged up at the same time he drew her down until he could claim her mouth. It was not only the best way he'd ever found to quiet her, but she also tasted so damn good.

Her tongue sparred with him just as much as her words had. But this was the kind of argument he could get behind. And he wouldn't even care if he lost.

After several seconds he let go, sprawling beneath her. Above him, Piper's pale blue eyes flashed a fire that he felt burning through his own belly. She watched him, her chest heaving as they both tried desperately to find some equilibrium.

But he was finally starting to realize there wasn't any equilibrium where Piper was concerned.

"Piper, if you don't want this then get up and walk away right now."

Stone tried to do the right thing by letting go, but his fingers wouldn't listen. Instead of releasing his hold on her hips, his grip tightened. "In about thirty seconds I'm going to strip the rest of that bikini down your body and not stop until we're both begging for mercy."

He might have missed her silent gasp if he hadn't been watching every subtle shift of her body. Her shoulders jerked with the motion of it and her breasts swayed, taunting, tempting.

He waited for her sanity to save them both. But instead of pushing away, Piper shifted closer, spreading her thighs wide across his hips. The hot cradle of her sex settled over the hard ridge of his desire for her.

Dropping to her elbows, she flattened the luscious curve of her breasts against his chest. Leaning close, she found his ear and whispered, "Promises, promises," at the same time her hips rolled.

And Stone was pretty damn certain the world erupted in a shower of sparks raining fire across his skin.

Grasping Piper by the waist, he picked her up and flipped them both so she was beneath him.

"No fair," she groused.

"Sweetheart, I haven't been with a woman for ten years and I've wanted you for every one of them. Longer. My control is razor-thin."

The harsh edge of need pulling at her features disappeared. "Dammit," she breathed out, and reached for him. Her fingers smoothed his hair back from his face, tangling in the strands and gently drawing him close.

His mouth touched hers. Heat simmered through the connection as he savored the feel of her soft lips.

He drank her in, relishing the sigh of pleasure she gave him.

But he wasn't satisfied with that taste of her. "I want all of you."

His lips trailed across her skin, down her throat, over her collarbone and the soft swell of her upper breast. The tips of her nipples puckered into rosy buds that beckoned him to suck deeply.

With the tip of his tongue, he drew an ever-tightening swirl, closer and closer. Her back arched and her hold on his hair tightened, urging him where she wanted him to touch.

And the whole time she watched him, blue eyes glittering with a maddening combination of fire and ice.

He couldn't take his eyes off of her and the attention was rewarded when his teeth finally tightened over the nub of her breast. He sucked, deep and hard. A whimper fell from her lips. Her eyes closed and her head rolled back.

And he almost exploded at the sight of her bliss.

But it still wasn't enough.

He moved farther down her body, using his mouth to give little nips and kisses along the way. Sucking at the taut skin just below the band of her bikini bottoms until a pink mark appeared. Relishing the way she writhed beneath him, her body searching out more of what he was giving her.

Snagging his fingers in the waistband, he dragged the small triangle of material down her legs, exposing all of her to him. Tossing them aside, Stone stood at the end of the chaise and stared at her.

"You're gorgeous," he finally breathed.

Grasping her thighs, Stone used his grip to pull her down the chaise. Dropping to his knees, he didn't even feel the sting of stone as he draped her thighs over his shoulders and spread her wide.

All he could see was the perfection of her sex, glistening wet with the evidence of her need for him. The scent of her was hot and heady and made the blood pound harder through his veins.

Diving in, Stone took a single lap of her, humming in the back of his throat. Her hips lifted, chasing after his mouth. Placing a palm on her belly, he held her in place, knowing they were both going to enjoy this ride. Dropping his thumb down beside the tight bundle of nerves at the top of her sex, Stone gave her clit a couple quick strokes before going in for more.

This time he relished, lapping and sucking, using his entire mouth to give her pleasure.

The first orgasm startled them both. It hit so hard and quick that Piper's entire body bucked under the force of it. And all Stone could think was that he'd never get enough of this.

Of her.

Piper was pretty certain the world had tilted on its axis. Or at least her world had.

She was twenty-eight. She'd had sex. Good sex. Or so she'd thought. Nothing compared to what

Stone had just shown her. With nothing more than his mouth.

She was in some serious trouble here.

Not that she cared at the moment.

Stone wrapped an arm around her and pulled her back up the chaise with him. Her body was limp, replete, and yet somehow still hungry.

She'd wanted this man for a very long time and what he'd given her was nowhere near enough.

Stone nuzzled at her throat. He rained kisses across her face. The warmth of his body stretched beside her was heaven. But for the first time she realized she was completely naked and he still had on shorts and a button-down. How had that happened?

And what was she going to do about it?

Fingers playing with the buttons on his shirt, it didn't take her long to figure it out. Popping the top disc through the little hole, Piper let her gaze trail down the strong column of his throat. The urge to lean forward and press her lips to his skin, to lick and absorb the salty taste of him, was overwhelming.

It wasn't a foreign sensation. It was something she'd thought many times, back then and now. Suddenly, Piper realized she didn't have to force herself not to give in.

The freedom of that realization made her dizzy.

Fingers brushing the tangle of hair away from her face, Stone ducked his head until his gaze snagged hers again. "What are you thinking? That sexy brain of yours is whirling so fast I can practically hear it."

Piper licked her lips. A tangled knot of sensations coiled in her belly, chief among them trepidation. Considering just moments ago the man had had his face buried in her sex that seemed like an asinine reaction. But there it was.

Old habits died hard and the thought of being honest with him about her feelings now felt like taking a giant leap out of a soaring airplane…without a parachute.

"I wanted to taste your throat."

"Ooookay." Stone drew out the single word. "Explain why that would make smoke pour out of your ears."

"Because I've wanted to do that and more to you since I was fifteen. Thirteen years is a long time for you to star in my fantasies. I'm still a little shell-shocked I finally have the chance for it to be real."

"To be fair, I wasn't exactly accessible for ten of those."

Piper slammed her palms into his chest and shoved. "Jerk," she said, the laughter she couldn't quite deny ringing through the single word. "You think just because I couldn't see you, touch you or talk to you that I forgot about you? That I stopped wanting you? Needing you? Caring about you?"

Stone rolled to his back, pulling her with him. His hands wrapped around her wrists, holding her in place above him.

"I'd hoped."

Gone was the playful tone they'd shared a few moments ago. Now he stared up at her, earnest, his tawny eyes full of regret that she never, ever wanted to see again. A lump formed in the back of her throat and not for the first time, Piper wanted to scream.

To yell at the sky until someone answered back and explained why life had to be so unfair.

But there wasn't an answer. Because it just was.

It was her turn to brush soft fingers across his cheek. To lean close and whisper, "You're a fool," before locking her mouth with his.

The taste of him exploded through her, as it always did, filling her up. The rough texture of his shirt abraded her skin, a contrast to the weight of his hand as it settled against the small of her back. His touch reminded her that she was naked. And she wanted him that way, too.

Making quick work of the buttons on his shirt, Piper spread it wide. And nearly swallowed her tongue. She knew he'd grown a ton of muscles since she last saw him…but the up close and personal view had her pulse fluttering.

And had her fantasizing about running her tongue across every peak and valley of his pecs and abs.

"Breathe, baby." Stone chuckled. Folding one arm behind his head, he stretched his body to give her an even better view of…everything.

A rueful expression crossed Piper's face. "Cocky bastard."

His response was a half shrug. Followed by a roll of his hips that managed to prove he had plenty to be cocky about when the hard length of his erection ground against her hip.

Her sex instinctively clenched, which made her both irritated and weak at the knees. Piper didn't particularly enjoy being a slave to anything, including her own libido.

But two could play that game.

Raising an eyebrow, Piper threw one leg over his hips, but didn't settle over him as she knew he expected. Instead, she stayed up on her knees, reaching high for the sky and giving a little stretch of her own.

"Piper," he growled, in warning. Although, she wasn't entirely certain what he was trying to warn her about.

The soft sea breeze kissed her skin, mixing with the warmth of the sunlight. Leaning back, she shook her head, enjoying the way her hair tickled across her skin. Not to mention the pinch of Stone's fingers wrapped around her hips.

Surging up, he wrapped his arms around her. Piper's body jerked as he brought her flush against him. The rough hair from his chest teased her already tightened nipples. And the rest of her just burned.

"You're playing with fire."

"God, I hope so," she taunted.

Stone twisted his fingers deep into her hair. Not pulling, but letting her feel the strength he was using to hold back. His mouth latched onto her shoulder, teeth nipping, lips sucking.

Reaching between them, Piper found the zipper on his shorts and yanked it open. The backs of her fingers brushed against the long length of him and she drank in his tortured hiss.

His arms wrapped around her. Crushed her. So close, she could feel the frenzy of desire running beneath his skin. Wanted to soothe him. Give him anything that would make it better.

Her entire body thrummed with the need of him.

Freeing his erection, Piper let her fingers absorb the texture of him. Learn this piece of him that she'd never had before. Fisting him, she let her palm slip up and down the hot length of him.

Satin over steel. Hard and pulsing. Piper relished the way his hips jerked with each pump of her tight fist around him. She wanted to feel him deep inside her, stroking and rubbing and grinding against her.

But he didn't give her very long to play before he growled, "Baby, stop. I'm not coming in your hand."

Yeah, that's not what she wanted either.

Pushing up with her knees for leverage, Piper positioned him at the entrance to her sex. Before he could react, her body was sliding down over him, taking him in.

"Goddammit," he breathed out, his grip on her hips digging hard.

Piper's head fell back. She reveled in the sensation of having him fill her up. Her body stretched to accept him, a delicious burn that she'd feel in the morning. And remember.

The throb of her own heartbeat centered at her sex, a tattoo of need only Stone could soothe. Beneath her, his entire body vibrated, but even fully seated, he didn't move.

Instead, he pulled back, putting just enough space between them so that he could look deeply into her eyes.

The world stilled, or it felt that way. The pull of the moon might have kept the tide moving and the earth spinning, but Piper didn't feel it. Didn't register anything except Stone and the intensity focused solely on her.

She couldn't untangle the emotions swirling through his eyes, but then she wasn't sure what she was feeling herself. Elation, trepidation, hope, sadness, inevitability.

She'd had sex, multiple times. She'd experienced intimacy, or so she'd thought. But there was something so raw about the way Stone stared at her.

And she wasn't sure she was ready to deal with being that *naked*. Not yet. Not even with him.

Closing her eyes, Piper dropped her forehead against his and breathed deep.

"Birth control?" he asked.

"What?"

"Are you on birth control?" Stone grit out. "I'm not wearing a condom."

"Yes."

"I saw Dr. Phillips when I got out and had a battery of tests. I'm clean."

"Good to know. I am, too."

That was all it took to have his hips surging up and leaving her words to break away into nothing. She couldn't speak. Or think. Just feel.

Piper used what leverage she had to rock against him, timing the surge and release of her thighs with the thrust and retreat of Stone's cock. Their bodies slipped together, rubbed and connected. Found a rhythm that made the world fade.

His grip on her hips controlled the pace, slowing her just when she wanted to race. Together, they panted, their mouths meeting and mingling in kiss after kiss.

A sob of need built deep inside her chest. Pressure desperate for release.

And then it was there. The orgasm exploded through her, wringing a cry that sounded very much like "Stone" from her lips.

The world blacked out, possibly because she forgot how to breathe. And she drifted, enjoying the tiny aftershocks that rocked through her body.

What called her back was the sound and sensation of Stone's orgasm. Piper's eyes popped open and there he was, filling her vision.

His glorious body was drawn tight, covered in a sheen of sweat. Deep inside, she felt the kick of him. The shudder that rocked through him. Leaning forward, she pressed her mouth to his, drinking in his groan of relief mixed with the sweet sound of her name.

That had absolutely been worth the wait.

Stone collapsed onto the chaise. Their arms and legs were a tangle that neither had the energy to unravel. Beside her, his chest heaved as he tried to catch his breath. And a happy smile played across Piper's swollen lips.

Leaning up on her elbow, she peered down at him.

He was gorgeous. With a light touch, she swept a strand of hair off his forehead.

His eyes cracked open, glinting at her in the sunlight. Happiness bubbled up inside her. It should have scared her, how consuming and gigantic the sensation was.

But it didn't.

Sweeping the pad of her finger across his parted lips, she grinned down at him. "Well, you certainly haven't forgotten how to do that."

Eleven

She deserved to have her ass smacked for that comment, but he was too exhausted right now.

Stone dragged her backward with him. A few minutes. That's all he needed to gather his strength after she'd completely wrung him out.

Then he'd pick her up. Get her out of the sun so her skin wouldn't burn more. And if he was lucky, he'd be able to sweet-talk her into round two.

Although, given her vocal reaction to what they'd just shared, he didn't think much convincing would be required.

Piper tucked her head against his shoulder and settled against the curve of his body. He tried not to think about how perfectly she fit there. Right now, he wasn't going to look past the next several hours.

At the moment, he felt like his entire life had just been dumped on its head. The last time that had happened didn't exactly have a spectacular outcome.

"Why can I never stay mad at you?" Piper's fingers drew idle patterns across his chest.

Yeah, he might not have been around a woman for a while, but he wasn't dumb. He was smart enough to realize no answer to that question could lead anywhere good.

Leaning up on an elbow, Piper looked down at him. "I mean, you're high-handed, dictatorial and infuriating. You make my blood boil on a regular basis and have since we were little."

"I remember," Stone said, a rueful smile twisting his lips as he unconsciously touched the scar that ran up into his hairline. It was so faded now that even he had trouble finding it.

Piper's hand brushed his away, the cool pad of her index finger tracing the jagged line. She obviously knew right where it was, which shouldn't be surprising since she'd put it there.

"You always did have a temper."

Piper laughed. "That's funny. Not with anyone else. You always knew which of my buttons to push."

"Yeah, I did."

"You still do."

Grabbing her around the waist, Stone rolled until she was tucked beneath him and leered. "You gonna let me push them again?"

She smacked his shoulder, but couldn't quite stop

a smile from tugging at the corners of her lush lips. "Maybe."

"Oh, you're gonna let me touch all of them," he growled as his mouth found hers. He'd fought against wanting her for so long and now that he'd touched her, tasted her, claimed her...he had no intention of letting her go.

And the way she melted beneath him, her body going liquid and pliant, backed up the confidence he'd laced around the words. She wanted this as much as he did. He'd seen it, clear as day, deep inside those crystal-blue eyes as he'd stroked inside her.

To prove to them both just how right he was, Stone began to let his hands caress down the velvet softness of her skin. But right about the time his fingers brushed beside the dint of her belly button a large rumble erupted between them, startling the hell out of him.

And reminding him that his initial trip out here had been to tell Piper he'd made lunch.

Collapsing onto her back, Piper's body sagged beneath him, losing the taut awareness that had crept in when he'd started to explore.

"The expression on your face right now... I wish I had a camera."

"Ha ha, funny girl." Pushing to his feet, Stone wrapped his hand around her wrist and tugged until she followed him up. Reaching behind her, he snagged the flimsy dress she'd been wearing earlier, gathered it in his hands and pulled it on over her head.

His half-hard cock nearly wept when the material settled over her body, but his brain tried to reason that if he fed her now, they could enjoy hours of fun later.

Arm slung around her waist, he pulled her into the shelter of his body. "Food now, sex later."

Piper's hands splayed across his chest, but she didn't push him away. Instead, she settled against him, the sensation of her being in his arms so comfortable and *right*.

"Such a Neanderthal."

"Please. Your stomach would suggest you simply say thank you."

Turning out of his arms, she trotted away, tossing a taunting look over her shoulder. "Thank you."

Stone shook his head. Even when she did what he suggested she was always full of attitude. And he loved it.

Following behind her, Stone quickened his pace so he could catch up, and give her a sharp swat across her pert rear.

Piper yelped, stopped in her tracks and glared at him over her shoulder. "Try that again, stud, and we're going to have words."

Blood whooshed through his veins and he couldn't quite hold back the exhilaration that bubbled through him. One of the best things about Piper was the fact that she didn't let him intimidate her. Never had. Even as a slip of a little girl, she'd always acted like she was ten feet tall and bulletproof.

And it had been his job to protect her. To make sure she could continue to believe that.

He didn't deserve to touch all that fire. To call it his. And yet, here they were.

So, he was going to enjoy it while he had it.

Wrapping his arm around her shoulders, Stone pulled her against his body. Her back settled against his chest and her head immediately dropped to his shoulder, exposing her throat.

Whether she realized it or not, she'd just given him the most perfect gift. The gift of her trust. Her vulnerability.

"Sweetheart," he rumbled, low and deliberate against her ear. "The next time your ass tingles from my handprint you're going to be panting and begging me to come."

She laughed, the bleat of sound incredulous. "I seriously doubt that."

A slow smile curled at the corners of his lips. "Care to make a bet?"

A shiver rocked down her spine, rubbing the round curve of her ass right against his erection that was suddenly very far from semi.

Yep, he had no doubt she was going to enjoy this. But first, he had to feed her.

Piper was on edge, and it was surprising considering not two hours ago she'd been limp from two very delicious orgasms.

It was all Stone's fault.

She'd never been the kind of woman greedy for orgasms before. She'd dated guys. Been in relationships. Sex was pleasant. She enjoyed it.

She did not crave it.

Not like this.

The need for more didn't cloud every thought or prevent her from carrying an intelligent conversation.

Maybe it was just because it was new.

Or maybe it was just because it was Stone and she'd wanted him for so long.

Whatever it was, she needed to find a cure because she was becoming seriously irritated with herself.

Leaning back in his chair, Stone sipped from the glass of wine he'd poured and watched her across the table tucked into the breakfast nook beside the kitchen. The space was intimate, certainly more so than the formal dining room she'd seen last night when she was wandering the house.

They'd been talking for a while. Stone asking all sorts of questions about her life—the part he'd missed—and her only having enough functioning brain cells at the moment to answer.

She'd spent that time watching his mouth move. The way his strong fingers caressed the cool stem of his glass. It had really done a number on her when he'd gathered a drop of condensation rolling down the side onto his finger and sucked it into his mouth.

Everything inside her had gone molten. What the hell was wrong with her? She was long past the point of out-of-control hormonal reactions to the opposite sex.

Humor, heat and intense interest filled Stone's gaze as he watched her. "Piper."

"Yeah." She really needed to get a grip. Maybe getting him to talk would do the trick. "Tell me about being inside."

Piper wanted to know, but she also needed him to share that piece of himself with her. Needed it in a way that was more demanding even than the sexual haze currently distracting her.

"Tell me," she said again when he didn't react.

She knew he wouldn't want to. Understood the reasons behind his inevitable protest. And she was ready for them. Had formulated her argument against just about anything he could say.

This wasn't something she'd decided in the last two hours. It was something she'd realized days ago. After their first encounter in his parents' library. She just didn't think there would be an opportunity where he might be open to sharing.

And maybe this wasn't the time, but right now, she needed to know if he was open. Before she let herself get in too deep.

If she wasn't already.

What she wasn't prepared for was for him *not* to argue. For him to simply give her what she'd asked for. Or at least some of what she'd asked for.

"It wasn't fun, but it's prison so it wasn't sup-posed to be."

Piper schooled her reaction. Pulling her prac-ticed, professional composure from deep inside, she wrapped it around herself like a familiar blanket. And let him continue.

"You haven't met Gray or Finn, but I'm sure you will."

Piper tried not to let the inevitability and acceptance in that statement mean too much. But it was difficult.

"I never expected to find two men who mattered to me in prison. I mean, I'm a criminal, but we both know the circumstances surrounding my plea deal."

Guilt snaked through Piper's belly. Her composure slipped, apparently enough for Stone to see it because he said, "Don't you dare. You know that's not what I meant. I've said this before, and I'll say it again. Every day if you need to hear it. I've never regretted the decisions I made. And I never will.

"What I meant was it's not like I'm a typical criminal. And trust me, the other inmates were fully aware of who I was the moment I walked in the place. If there's one thing I learned, it was that the gossip inside is worse than anything you'd find in the worst middle school. Because no one has anything else to occupy their time."

Oh, she could imagine. But it bothered her that even in prison, Stone had endured people whispering about him. Had speculated and passed judgment over him without having the first clue about the man he truly was.

It pissed her off that the entire world was still doing that.

But that was a conversation for another time.

"My plan was to keep to myself, avoid confrontation and serve out my time." The bitter edge to his laughter sent a shiver of apprehension through Piper.

"The other inmates had a different idea. I might have been in a low-security prison, but it was still filled with criminals. And they didn't particularly like the idea that a convicted murderer, one they felt had bought his way into a lighter sentence and had billions in the bank, was among them. And they set out to prove—to themselves and me—that I was no better than they were."

"Dammit," Piper breathed. Her chest ached. She could imagine the boy he'd been, twenty and unfamiliar with the rough side of the world, even if his parents hadn't always sheltered him, confronting men who had something to prove and a mean streak that ran deep enough to inflict pain.

"I'm sorry." The words weren't nearly enough, but it was all she could do.

"Nope, not your responsibility to apologize, Piper."

Her jaw ground against the unfairness of what he'd just said. "Maybe not, but you're getting it anyway. You might not wish anything was different, but I do. I spent ten years closing my eyes at night, hoping when I opened them it would all be just a nasty dream. That somehow I could figure out a way to change it. To fix it. And you telling me I shouldn't feel that way is wrong, Stone. You don't get to make that determination for me. For anyone."

He shrugged. "I hear you."

But he didn't agree with her. Not the first time—or most likely the last—they'd have to agree to disagree.

"Through all of that though, I found Gray and Finn. They were outcasts just like I was. At first, we banded together because there's strength in numbers. But eventually, we earned each other's respect. And trust. They're honorable—well, Finn is honorable in his own way. And I'd trust them with my life. Have on more than one occasion.

"It didn't take us long to realize none of us was weak. We might not have had the physical strength some of the other inmates did—"

"At first," she drawled, lifting a single eyebrow as her gaze pointedly traveled across the expanse of naked chest beneath the open shirt he'd pulled on before coming inside.

"At first," he acknowledged, humor crinkling the edges of his eyes.

"I'd spent years studying business. I was practically raised in a boardroom. Our dinner table conversation not only covered grades and school assignments, but discussion of material costs, negotiation tactics and bargaining power. Once I figured out that even behind bars the world runs on currency and power…it was simply a matter of figuring out the business I wanted to run."

"I bet the guards loved you."

"They did. They liked the Cuban cigars I had shipped in for their weekly poker game. Not to mention the fact that I kept a tight lid on what I could and made their jobs easier."

Yeah, she didn't doubt that at all. Stone might have become some prison boardroom badass, but he was still the same man he'd always been, down to his core—strong, honorable and determined.

"So, the first few months were rough. One of the reasons I'd only let my dad visit was because I knew my mom would freak if she saw my face." The ghost of pain mixed with humor in his eyes.

"Is that why you wouldn't let me come?"

And just like that the humor fled, leaving only the pain behind. The sharpness of it had breath backing up into her lungs. She wasn't going to like what he had to say.

"No. I never intended to let you come. Piper, I didn't want you within a thousand yards of that place."

"But you were going to let your mom visit?"

"No." His mouth twisted. "Yes. It's different."

"I don't see how." Hadn't they already tread over this ground? And, yet, it seemed they were going to continue having the exact same conversation. "Stone, you killed him. For me. I just don't understand how you could cut me out after that."

"I killed him. For you. And I was glad, Piper. I didn't have a single moment of regret. Not a spark. I'm pretty certain that makes me a monster."

"I'm pretty certain that makes you a hero. My hero, in this case. But you can't tell me if you'd walked in on that same scene, with Blaine attacking another woman, that you wouldn't have reacted the same way. Because you would have. Because you're a good guy. You do the right thing. No matter what the cost. And you always have."

It was one of the reasons she loved him.

But those words stuck in her throat when what she really wanted to do was share them.

"It doesn't matter."

"Somehow, I think it does. But, I forgive you."

"Oh, yeah? How magnanimous of you." His eyes glittered at her, anger and irritation turning them to polished stone.

"Don't be an asshole. Do you think I could have shared what we just shared outside if I didn't? I forgive you for cutting me out, and trust me, a huge part of me would like to stay mad at you. That hurt. Deeply. But I also forgive you for doubting me. For thinking me weak, and then treating me like I am. I forgive you for making decisions about my life without consulting me. But mostly, I forgive you for not asking for my forgiveness about any of that and not even understanding why you should."

She forgave him?

Well, wonderful for her. But he didn't forgive himself.

He'd done something terrible. His soul was stained with the reality, but worse, he was so afraid that stain would bleed onto her. And he'd do anything to prevent that from happening.

He'd fought to keep her at arm's length because he didn't deserve her. Plain and simple.

He'd forgotten that for a little while.

Pushing away from the table, Stone walked away. He needed distance, from her and from the emotions this conversation was dragging up.

But she wasn't about to let him get away. Not this time. Instead, Piper followed as he paced into the living room. He stopped at the wall of windows, facing the gorgeous vista of tropical paradise spread in front of him.

And he wanted to scream.

How could the world look perfect and beautiful and yet still be capable of holding so much pain?

Her soft hands landed on his hips. The heat of her body seeped into him as she pressed close. She didn't say anything, but simply stood there. His breath raced inside his lungs. Her arms wrapped around him from behind, hands pressed against his chest as if she could hold his galloping heart.

Because that's what she'd want to do for him.

"I wasn't fast enough," he finally growled.

She shrugged. "Do you think I was asking for what happened? Taunted him?"

"No, of course not."

"I was wearing a tight skirt and a shirt that showed my belly that night," she murmured.

Stone shook his head, not understanding. Turning, he said, "What does that have to do with anything?"

"I didn't scream no. I didn't make any noise at

all really. At first I was too shocked, and then his hand was over my mouth. But maybe I didn't struggle enough."

She was starting to piss him off. "What?"

"Maybe that makes it my fault."

"Of course it doesn't."

"Mmm," she murmured, her arms tightening around him. "Then why do you insist on feeling guilty for something neither of us is responsible for?"

Stone stood still, her words slowly sinking in.

He wasn't responsible.

Logically, he recognized that. "I'd give anything to have been able to stop it sooner, Piper."

The warmth of her breath seeped into his chest. "Do you think I don't know that? Or wish things had been different in so many ways? What if I had screamed? Maybe someone else would have come running and you wouldn't have killed him, losing ten years of your life. But you don't have the capability of changing the past any more than I do."

She was right, but that knowledge didn't take away the frustration or the feeling of inadequacy. The regret that he hadn't acted sooner and the knowledge that he was damaged down to his core.

"You've given enough because of what happened. I don't need or expect you to give any more. You saved me, and I'll always be grateful. You spent years protecting me, but maybe now it's my turn to protect you."

"What do you mean?"

"I mean you've whisked me away to a Caribbean island, put both of our lives on hold, because you don't want me to tell anyone about what Blaine did. But maybe it's time to share the truth. To free us both from the weight of the past."

"No." The harsh word flew from his mouth. Nope, he wasn't going to let that happen.

"Stone, running away from your problems will never solve anything."

Oh, he was fully aware of that. "Thanks for the advice, Doc, but I'm not running. I'm strategically managing."

Piper laughed, the sound harsh. "We have a difference of opinion on that."

"Duly noted."

"Everything would be easier if you'd just let me tell Madelyn Black what happened."

Piper closed what little distance was between them, laying her hands on his chest. Tipping her head back, she stared into him with those ice-blue eyes that had owned him since he'd met her. When she was younger, he'd been powerless to deny her anything when she looked at him that way.

But not even that could make him agree to what she was suggesting.

"Let me tell the world you were protecting me. Please. I can't give you back the ten years, but let me do this for you. For us."

"No," he growled, not even bothering to stop long enough to think about it. "I sacrificed ten years of my life because protecting you from the weight of what would have come afterward was worth it. I couldn't prevent the rape, but I could make it so you didn't have to deal with reliving the experience. With explaining to your mom and Morgan what Blaine had done."

Placing his own palms over hers, Stone drew her even closer. "Telling the truth now would make those ten years pointless. And I don't think I could deal with that, Piper. I need them to matter."

Piper blanched. Her shoulders heaved on a big pull of air, like she couldn't get enough into her lungs.

"They matter," she whispered. "To me, they always will."

Her eyes closed, pausing for several seconds. Stone watched her gather strength. When she opened her eyes again, he could see the purpose and courage shining in them.

"I know what you did and why you did it. I was... shattered back then, although part of that was losing you. I might not have been able to handle the spectacle and trial then, but I can handle the scrutiny now. I've worked hard for the past ten years to find healing and peace. To find forgiveness and my own inner strength. Those ten years you sacrificed gave me that. Now I can do this. Free us. For you. For us."

Grasping his hands, Piper squeezed hard. "Please, let me."

Twelve

Something brushed against the back of Piper's neck. Moist heat. Soft lips. Languid warmth melted through her body. Stone's fingers swept down her spine before caressing across the curve of her rear.

Moonlight spilled into the room, bathing the bed in a silver glow. Neither one of them had bothered to close the blinds on the wall of windows when they'd gone to bed. Although, considering Stone had been pulling her clothes off as they went, that wasn't necessarily a surprise.

Piper had no idea what time it was, not that it mattered. She'd fallen asleep in Stone's arms, thinking there was no place she'd rather be. However, waking up there was ten times better. Especially with the kind of wake-up call Stone was giving her.

His hands kneaded her muscles, moving up and down her body, leaving her restless and loose at the same time. It was an unexpected sensation, made even more so when his lips joined in.

He trailed openmouthed kisses down the line of her spine. And then nipped at the flesh of her ass, drawing an unexpected gasp from her. Piper's legs scissored restlessly against the soft sheets.

She tried to flip over, but Stone's wide palm spread across the small of her back, holding her in place.

"Stone," she protested.

Leaning close, he whispered in her ear, "Let me touch you. Learn you."

How could she say no?

Letting her body sink deep into the mattress, Piper tumbled headlong into the pleasure Stone was building.

Sucking the lobe of her ear into his mouth, he tugged, creating an answering pulse between her thighs.

"Close your eyes," he murmured.

The moment she did, every one of her other senses kicked into overdrive. The scent of him, so familiar and tantalizing, surrounded her. Pulling in a deep breath, she held it, absorbed him.

The rough pads of his fingers brushed softly across her skin. He touched and teased, exploring every inch of her body in a way that was delicious and maddening. Especially when he nudged her thighs wide and followed the crease of her ass right up to the wet heat of her sex. But didn't actually touch where she needed him most.

The harsh sound of her own breathing echoed through Piper's skull.

She was done playing Stone's game.

Pushing up, she flipped over so she could see him. The intense expression on his face sent a violent shiver of need rocking through her body. The way he stared at her—as if he could see deep into her soul and connected with what he saw—made everything inside her unfurl.

No one had ever looked at her that way. Not even Stone. Until this moment, she didn't realize it was what she'd been missing. And not just because it was obvious in that moment that she was everything that mattered to him.

But because she felt the same way about him.

It wasn't sudden or surprising. It wasn't just sex, although they were clearly about to share in that. What she had with Stone went far deeper and always had.

It scared her. Because losing him again would be devastating.

Needing the taste of him on her lips, Piper grasped his face and pulled him in close, whispering, "Kiss me."

Stone didn't disappoint, but then he rarely did. He swooped in and claimed her mouth with the same intensity that had filled his eyes. It was overwhelming and perfect. Earth-shattering and somehow calming.

Because she knew. There was no one for her, but

Stone. They could spend ten more years apart and it would always be him.

Her hands raced across his body, tugging, teasing, touching. She wanted all of him. Needed all of him, right now. Desperation fueled her movements, but Stone wasn't having any of it.

He covered her hands, slowed her. Forcing her to drink in every sensation and savor it like the wine they'd shared with dinner last night.

"I'm not going anywhere," he murmured against her shoulder. With lazy licks, he dragged his tongue across her collarbone, stopping to suck at the underside of her jawline.

"I know," she panted out, her fingers still grasping at him, urging him for more.

Pulling away, Stone stared deep into her eyes and said again, "I'm not going anywhere."

A sound hiccuped from her lungs, startling Piper. Another followed and suddenly her cheeks were wet. Stone rained soft kisses across her face, sipping at the tears as they flowed. "I should stay far away from you, Piper. I don't deserve you in my life. But I can't do it. I'm not a good man."

Piper reared back and smacked her hand against his shoulder. "Stop saying that. You are."

"You know nothing of the things I've done."

"So tell me. But I promise whatever you share, it won't change a thing."

Stone simply shook his head. "The details aren't important. What is, is that you make me almost believe I can be a better person."

Piper grasped him. "You're amazing, Stone, just the way you are." Emotions welled inside her.

She wanted to give him the words, to voice what she knew was true deep down. But they wouldn't come. She was still scared. Scared that something else would come and take him away.

But for now, they were both there and she was going to take the gift they'd been given.

Stone's kisses changed. One moment they were soothing, the next demanding. And Piper met his demand. She arched into his body, relishing the way his hard muscles rubbed against her soft skin.

His fingers found the tender peak of her nipples and tugged. Gently at first, but then harder and harder until the burn of his touch wrung a gasp from her. Heat melted through her body, drawing her muscles tight in a silent demand for more. His tongue followed, a gentle lap that relieved the sharp edge he'd caused.

Rolling the tight bud, he sucked it deeply. Piper's body arched up off the soft surface of the bed, chasing after him. The moist heat of his mouth was heaven. "More," she demanded, although she wasn't entirely certain what she was asking for.

Stone understood though.

His teasing fingers swept down the length of her body, caressing her stomach, thighs and hips. He found her sex, wet and pulsing with her need for him. Stone dragged his fingers through the evidence of her desire, stroking deep. Piper's eyes closed on the sensation of bliss.

Stone teased, moving slow and driving her need steadily higher. Piper writhed beneath him.

"Please, Stone. Please. I need… I need…" She couldn't even get the words out. Or fully form the thought.

"I know, baby," he hummed straight into her ear.

Piper could feel her orgasm, oh, so close. With a few thrusts of her hips, she could have gone over. Wanted to. But wanted him with her more.

Grasping his hand, Piper pulled him up and over her. She spread her thighs and positioned the head of his thick sex at the entrance to her body. His gaze found hers as he thrust inside. Piper threw her head back, relishing the sensation of his hard cock stroking deep.

"Look at me," he growled.

Piper did, locking her gaze with his. Something about the power and depth of his expression reverberated through her. He pumped, once, twice and again. Every muscle in Piper's body went taut before the world exploded in a burst of ecstasy. Deep inside, she felt the kick of Stone's release.

His forehead dropped to hers. Their panting breaths mingled. But he kept hold of her gaze and refused to let her go.

Piper was caught. Trapped. But nothing inside her wanted to escape. In fact, she never wanted to move from right here, his sweat-slicked body next to hers.

Obviously, that wasn't an option.

Eventually, they'd have to move.

But for now…

* * *

Their last couple days had been blissful, full of sun and sand and sex. Lots of amazing sex. Piper's body was sore in the best way possible and her heart was happy. For the first time in her life, she contemplated the possibility that disappearing for a while might have merit.

As long as Stone was with her.

Rolling her head to the side, she took in the sight of him wearing nothing more than swim trunks that clung to his chiseled muscles and left her body buzzing. Piper let her gaze linger, drinking him in and relishing the fact that he was hers.

Always with a sixth sense when she was looking at him, Stone pulled the sunglasses hiding his tiger's-eye gaze down a half inch and gave her a cocky grin. "You know, you could come over here and do more than look."

"I'm pretty sure you were the one who suggested we needed a little break from the sexcapades."

Laughter burst out of him. "Sexcapades? Really, Doc? Is that a clinical term?"

She joined him in the laughter, letting the happiness of it bubble up inside her. "Maybe we should stay for another couple days."

Piper didn't understand why her words suddenly had the humor dying in his eyes. "As much as I'd love nothing better, I need to get back. I have a meeting with my parole officer, who doesn't exactly know I'm currently out of the country."

Jackknifing off the lounger, Piper said, "Excuse

me? You didn't tell your parole officer before leaving the country? Isn't that a violation worthy of sending you back? How the heck did we get through border control?"

"Honey, we both know money can buy almost anything."

Including entrance into a Caribbean island, apparently.

She was pissed. Only Stone could take her from bliss to fury in a nanosecond. "And why didn't you mention this before?"

"Because I knew you wouldn't be okay with it."

"Because it isn't okay, Stone." Rolling up from the chair, she stalked past him. Or tried to, but he reached out and snagged her wrist, pulling until she collapsed into his lap.

"Where do you think you're going?"

"To pack, so we can leave. Call to have the jet fueled or whatever you do."

"No."

"It really irritates me when you say that word."

"I'm aware."

"And, yet, you keep saying it."

"Because you keep suggesting things I don't want to do."

"Stone," she ground out between her teeth. "Be reasonable."

"I am," he said, slowly letting his hand slide up the inside of her thigh.

Piper slammed her legs together, trapping him before he could distract her enough that she'd forget what they were arguing about. "Oh, no you don't. That's not gonna work this time, buster."

Leaning close, he latched his teeth onto the tender part of her earlobe and tugged, murmuring, "Are you sure?"

No, no she wasn't. But she wasn't about to tell *him* that.

Crossing her arms over her chest, Piper willed herself not to succumb to his devious antics.

With a sigh, and an infuriating smile tugging at his delicious lips, Stone wrapped his arms around her body and pulled her into him. She kept herself rigid, her hard shoulder digging into his chest.

"At this point, it wouldn't make any difference. My meeting is tomorrow afternoon. We have plenty of time to get back and we've been gone for days. If someone was going to come looking for me, they would have already."

"Can't they do random drop-ins to check on you?"

"Yes, but Gray's had that covered. Trust me."

Goddammit. She hated when he used logic against her. It was really infuriating, especially when he made sense. Even if she'd never agree the decision he made was right. Letting her body relax against his, Piper settled into his hold.

"You're infuriating. And this is the kind of thing I keep talking about. You need to be up-front with me, Stone, or this isn't going to work. No keeping important information to yourself. Even if you think it's for my own good."

Piper expected a protest at the very least, so she

was surprised when Stone readily agreed. "I hear you. I didn't tell you when we first left because if you'll remember you weren't exactly in a reasonable frame of mind."

"For good cause."

He shrugged. "Noted."

Uncrossing her arms, Piper turned in his hold until she could find his mouth. The kiss was soft and easy, a connection and understanding she'd been craving for so long. A sigh escaped from her parted lips. Stone's hand fisted into her hair, gently holding her as he explored her mouth.

The white-hot passion that had been burning between them whenever they touched wasn't entirely gone, but in this moment it mellowed. Piper felt like she was drifting, sinking, relaxing into a warm river that she wanted to ride forever, with Stone.

She had no idea how long they kissed and touched, exploring without any pressure or purpose other than to discover the teasing touches that made each of them sigh with pleasure. But Piper was so pulled into the magic weaving between them that she wasn't aware of Stone's phone ringing until he pulled his mouth from her enough to answer.

"This better be important," he growled.

Draped across his body, Piper knew before he said anything that it was. Moments before, he'd been molten steel, malleable and strong beneath her. But suddenly his entire body vibrated with tension.

His arm wrapped around her, holding her close, as he surged up. In seconds they were both on their feet, Piper tucked tight against his side. Stone's fingers bit into her hip so hard she almost yelped, but the expression on his face kept her quiet.

"Send me the video. I'll have Piper take a look and see if she recognizes anything."

He nodded, as if the person on the other end of the line could see him. "No, I don't see any reason to return tonight. We'll be there in the morning as planned. Gray, thanks, man. I owe you one."

Punching the end-call button, Stone tossed his phone onto the chaise beside them. Piper watched it bounce and drop precariously close to the edge before settling. He didn't care; he was too busy glowering out at the Caribbean Sea. His jaw worked and Piper decided to just wait until he was ready to share.

It didn't take long.

"Someone broke into your place."

She didn't want to watch it, but she had to. And not just because Stone asked her to.

What Piper didn't expect was the resurrected feeling of being violated. She was far away and safe, but watching the shadowy figure creeping through her home… Yeah, it had sent a rush of cold through her body.

"Again," she forced herself to say.

The first time she'd simply been too stunned to concentrate on details. Squeezing her eyes tight, she tried to wade through the emotions churning inside so she could focus.

Stone clicked the play button, starting the dark,

grainy video again. Piper leaned forward, squinting to try and bring things more into focus.

It didn't really help.

The video had obviously been cut from what was most likely boring hours of absolutely nothing since she hadn't been home in days. She almost missed the first flash of movement. It looked so much like a shadow. If she didn't know there was nothing outside her front door that could have made the motion, she might have dismissed it completely.

"There." She pointed to the shifting degrees of dark gray on the screen. "Whoever it is, is outside the door."

Within seconds, her front door swung slowly in. The burglar was careful not to open it any wider than necessary. And closed it again immediately once inside.

Crouched down and hunched over, it was difficult to tell just how tall the person might be.

"Come on, stand up," she whispered, but they definitely didn't hear her.

They were wearing a bulky sweatshirt with a deep-cowled hood pulled so the material hung practically halfway down their face.

Piper watched, the camera on-screen switching from room to room, following the culprit. Twisting and turning, they skulked through her home like a malevolent ghost. But didn't really stop to assess or take any of her possessions.

Because they weren't there to steal.

"Nothing was taken," she said. Not a question, but a certain fact.

Stone answered her anyway. "No."

They were looking for information.

Or for her.

But most likely information since she couldn't for the life of her guess what anyone could gain from taking or hurting her.

"You realize this was probably some paparazzo hoping to find a juicy secret they could sell to the highest bidder," she murmured.

"Probably."

"Too bad my sex toy collection is stashed inside a locked box in the back of my closet."

His chest pressed against her back, where he'd taken up a protective position in case she needed his physical support—which she did. Piper felt Stone's stunned reaction. And then the slide of his body against her as he melted into silent laughter.

Well, that was something.

Leaning into him even more, Piper said, "There's nothing there for them to find."

"I didn't think there would be."

Together, they watched until the video froze on the darkened picture of her empty foyer.

"Anything?"

She really wanted to say yes. To provide some detail that could help figure out who had violated her personal space and put a stop to the invasion of their lives. But nothing about the figure had seemed familiar.

"No."

"It couldn't have been the reporter you spoke to?"

Piper heard the echo of Stone's anger and the censure in his words, but chose not to address them. They'd already been over that argument. More than once. And nothing new could come from having it again. What was done was done.

"It could have been. But it could be anyone, Stone. I mean, I can't even judge their height."

Frustration poured off him as he paced away from her. "Gray has someone running calculations to see if we can figure out height."

"You can do that? Even though they're crouching?"

"Forensics and mathematics are both amazing fields. You'd be surprised what you can estimate with a few strategic measurements. It's just not something that happens quickly."

"That's amazing. And a little scary."

Stone laughed, a sharp edge to the sound. "Tell me about it."

"Why do you know so much about this stuff?"

"Let's just say I developed an interest inside. And have cultivated friendships with people who know how to use the information to help those who sometimes can't help themselves."

There was a story there, but one Piper instinctively knew Stone wasn't in the right frame of mind to share with her at the moment. There'd be plenty of time for her to ask later.

Stepping close, she rolled onto her toes so she

could cup his face. His arm automatically wrapped around her waist, pulling her into his body.

"Why doesn't it surprise me?"

"What?"

"Do you think I don't see you, Stone? That I don't know you down to your marrow? Only you could spend ten years in jail and pick up all this knowledge with the intent of helping people who can't help themselves. You have a savior complex, Mr. Stone. And while there are days that reality rubs me the wrong way, there are more days when I'm thankful for the selfless, honorable, caring man you are."

He stared at her for several seconds before using his leverage to bring her mouth to his. The kiss was comfortable and deep.

They stood together, soaking in the moment. Piper pulling strength, comfort and support from Stone even as she gave it back to him in the form of her acceptance and understanding.

And then he had to go and ruin the moment.

"You know I'm going to remind you of this the next time you get mad at me for doing something without asking you."

Thirteen

"Where are you taking me?"

And here, he'd hoped Piper's pleasant, accommodating mood would last more than a few hours.

Stone supposed he really shouldn't complain considering they'd had the best sex of his life last night. He'd never felt so connected to anyone as he'd felt when he'd been buried deep inside Piper's body as they'd come together.

Fifteen minutes inside the car that had met them at the airport and that malleability was toast.

"We're going to my place," he said.

"No, we're not."

"Piper, someone broke into your place."

"I'm perfectly aware of that, Stone. You were with me as we watched the video. Several times."

He stared at her, truly at a loss. "So, what did you expect me to do?"

It was an honest question. Piper was a brilliant woman. He didn't understand how she couldn't have come to the same conclusion he had—which was that her home wasn't safe right now, so there was no way on God's green earth he was taking her there. But especially not taking her there and dropping her off by herself since he had a meeting to go to.

"Nothing." Piper huffed. "Dammit. Exactly what you're doing."

Stone blinked and watched as Piper's ice-blue eyes flashed fire at him. Maybe silence was the smart choice here.

"But you have to start talking to me about things that affect my life, Stone. You can't keep making decisions without discussion."

Tilting his head, Stone studied her. Nope, she was absolutely serious.

"Piper, you're one of the most intelligent people I've ever met."

"Flattery will not solve this, Stone."

"That's good, but my statement wasn't flattery. It was fact. It never occurred to me that you'd come to any conclusion other than you couldn't go home. If you couldn't go home, then of course you'd come to my place."

She threw her hands up in the air. "Because we haven't talked about me coming over and staying. I've never even seen your place. I could stay with Mom and Morgan."

"We might have only been sleeping together for a few days, but we both know this isn't a brand-new relationship. There's no way I'd let you out of my sight—or my bed—under normal circumstances, let alone knowing someone is hell-bent on invading your privacy. And I don't think your mom would appreciate me having a go at you on her kitchen counter."

Piper blinked at him. His lips twitched as he watched the conflicting emotions chase across her face. Her pupils dilated with the memory of him doing just that in the kitchen at the house on the island.

But she was also still irritated with him.

After several seconds, Piper let her body sag against the soft seat. "God, I hate it when you're right."

Snagging her, Stone pulled her against him. "I know. Trust me, the feeling is mutual when that big brain of yours puts me in my place. But you know one of the things I love about us is the way you challenge me. Not many people do."

"Bull. I've seen you and Gray. He challenges you."

"Which is why he's my friend."

Pulling up outside his building, Stone brought her upstairs to his penthouse apartment. The property had come on the market while he was still in prison, but he'd wanted it so he'd bought it a couple years ago. The building had history, built in the early turn of the twentieth century. The space was massive, but the wraparound terrace with unobstructed views of the entire city were what sold him.

The place had been too big for him, something Finn had delighted in pointing out. But Stone hadn't cared. And as he watched Piper's reaction, he realized the decision had been right.

She immediately walked through his living room to the wall of floor-to-ceiling windows, taking in the view of Charleston. Looking over her shoulder, she breathed, "This is beautiful."

"And close to your office."

She just shook her head and tossed him a crooked smile, letting him win that point without comment.

"Make yourself at home. The kitchen should be stocked and your bag already in the master bedroom. I won't be long. Back in a couple hours."

His meeting with the parole officer shouldn't take more than one, but he wanted to swing by and check in with Gray while he was out.

From the doorway, Stone took her in. She looked so perfect in his home. No, *she* made it a home. Before, it was just an expensive piece of property. Crossing the space, Stone tried to swallow down his heart, which had somehow managed to jump up into his throat. Wrapping his arms around her waist, he pulled her body against his.

"Promise me you won't leave." He felt her body stiffen, but he didn't wait for the expected protest. "Just until I have a chance to talk with Gray and Morgan's security team. I'm still not satisfied with the answer for how the intruder got past them and into your place."

She stood in the circle of his arms for several seconds before finally letting out a sigh. "Fine. I won't leave."

Fingers under her chin, Stone tipped her head back and pressed his lips to hers, murmuring, "Thank you."

Piper prowled Stone's house. She called it that because as beautiful as it was, it didn't feel like a home. Yet. Not that he'd really had time to make it his own. But the space was gigantic, perfectly decorated and barren of anything personal that stamped the place as his. It was clear to her someone else had picked out the furniture and accessories…and not simply because he'd been unavailable when the property was purchased.

Once the hoopla died down, she'd help him make it his own.

In the meantime though, she was going bananas stuck in the ginormous space. Her footsteps echoed off the walls for God's sake. So when her phone rang, Piper snatched it up and answered without looking. Even a telemarketer would be someone to talk to for a few minutes.

"Piper! I've been worried sick about you. Where have you been? Even your mom didn't know." Carina's lilting voice had an edge of accusation Piper probably deserved.

"I'm sorry. Everything happened so quickly. I've been with Stone."

"What? What do you mean? Where were you and why didn't your mother know?" Carina's rapid-fire questions shot down the line.

Carina was asking questions that Piper couldn't fully answer without raising more. It would be like pulling a single thread and unraveling an entire sweater, especially with Carina. Her friend liked to dig.

Right now, Piper had a decision to make. She could lie to her best friend and continue to keep her in the dark. Continue to keep details secret about an event that had impacted not only Piper's life, but Carina's, as well. Or she could tell her the truth. But in telling her the truth, she was going to have to be fully honest with her.

She was going to have to share the secret she'd been keeping for so long.

On one hand, Carina had a right to know. Blaine's death had affected her life in so many ways. She deserved the truth.

But would sharing it with her destroy the memory she had of the man she loved? Was it right for Piper to do that?

But how could Piper look Stone in the eyes and tell him that being honest with the world was the right thing to do if she wasn't ready to be honest with the people who were closest to her?

Piper was so tired of living with the secret. Of

letting Stone shoulder the blame and responsibility when it wasn't his to take.

She understood his need to keep the information out of the media, even if she didn't agree with it. But sharing her own truth with Carina didn't mean they had to tell the world if Stone didn't want to. Carina was family. This was her decision, but that was his.

"It's a long story," she finally answered. "Too long over the phone. Why don't you come over and I'll explain everything?"

"Where are you?"

"Stone's place."

There was a long pause before Carina said, "I'll be there in twenty."

Piper texted her the address and then spent the next twenty minutes opening a bottle of wine—something told her they were both going to need it—and pulling out some snacks that she was too nervous to actually eat.

But she needed a task to occupy her mind.

Even though she was expecting it, she jumped when the front desk buzzed up to let her know Carina was there. Telling Dennis to send Carina up made her stomach jump into her throat. And no matter how often she swallowed, it simply wouldn't go down.

Was she making a mistake?

But the minute she opened the door and saw her friend standing there, an expression of concern on her face, Piper was certain this was the right thing to do.

Reaching out, Piper wrapped Carina in a warm hug and pulled her inside. "I'm so glad you're here."

Pushing back, Carina stared at her for several seconds before saying, "You're worrying me, Piper. What's going on?"

Ushering her over to the massive sofa, Piper handed her friend a glass of chilled wine, waved to indicate Carina should sit and then settled her own body into the corner of the soft leather couch. Taking a single sip, Piper set the glass aside and folded her hands into her lap. She definitely wasn't used to being the one talking in these situations and it left her feeling uncomfortable and out of her element.

"Stone and I were at his family's Caribbean island."

"Are you seeing him?"

Piper shook her head. Because she wasn't just seeing him. "I'm in love with him."

Saying the words out loud for the first time released a band of pressure she hadn't even realized had been constricting her chest.

She was in love with him.

Had been for as long as she could remember. And no matter what happened between her and Stone, nothing would ever change that truth. And she didn't ever want it to.

Carina's face flushed hot. Piper waited…expecting consternation or an accusation of betrayal. But none came. Instead, Carina took a slow, deliberate sip of her own wine and then followed suit by placing it on the glass-topped table beside them. "I don't know what to say. There's a huge part of me that's upset and hurt. But I recognize that isn't entirely fair. With anyone else I'd say this is fast, but something tells me it really isn't."

"No, no it isn't."

"You were close. Before." It wasn't a question, but a statement of fact. One that Carina had already known through her relationship with Blaine. Piper and Carina hadn't socialized together before, but they'd been aware of each other.

"Yes."

"Help me understand how you can love a murderer. What happened? Did Blaine's death cause problems between you?"

Piper swallowed. Part of her wished for the glass in her hand again, but it probably wouldn't help her desert-dry throat anyway. And she needed a clear head.

"Yes, and no." She licked her lips, a surge of uncertainty and fear rolling through her belly. Was this the right thing to do? Yes, it was. For Carina, for her and for Stone. Piper opened her mouth and let the rush of words she'd been holding back for ten years finally flow free. "Stone walked in on Blaine raping me ten years ago. He accidentally killed Blaine protecting me."

Carina blanched, her face going ghost white. Her eyes bugged wide. And then they began to glitter with the sheen of tears.

Piper waited as she watched emotions chase across her friend's face—disbelief, anger, pain, sorrow. Finally, Carina whispered, "I'm so sorry."

Piper had half expected an explosion of anger, denial. Had been emotionally prepared for it. What she'd never anticipated was this.

Piper shifted, moving next to Carina so she could place a comforting hand on her knee. "Sorry? You have nothing to apologize for."

"Maybe not, but that doesn't mean it doesn't hurt, knowing you went through something so traumatic."

"I know you never saw that side of Blaine. I also didn't want to ruin your memory of him…but you deserve to know the truth. To understand what really happened."

Carina glanced away, focusing on the plants and foliage on the patio just outside the door. Piper let her take all the time she needed to gather her thoughts. After several minutes, Carina shifted, her gaze locking once more onto Piper's.

"No, what you're describing doesn't match the Blaine I knew. But I'm aware he wasn't always the same with other people as he was with me. I never would have anticipated he could do something like you're describing. But he wasn't always a nice man."

Piper processed her words, letting them sink in. None of what Carina said came as a surprise. Piper had always known Blaine was an expert at showing people the face he wanted them to see. A master manipulator.

But Piper had to ask, "You believe me?"

"Of course I do. You have no reason to lie to me. And, this answers so many questions. Things I never understood finally make sense."

"I'm so sorry for keeping this from you for so long, but I wasn't ready to talk about it and Stone didn't want me to share the truth. Morgan doesn't even know."

"Are you going to tell him? Your mom?"

Piper wanted to. A tight knot formed in the pit of her belly at the thought. But again, the decision was hers.

"Yes, I plan to."

Carina nodded. "Why now?"

"Because I'm tired of living like I'm ashamed of what happened. I'm tired of people judging Stone when all he was doing was protecting me. Saving me. I need to do this so the two of us have a shot at moving forward and making our relationship work. I'm afraid if we don't, the poison that Blaine put into both of our lives will eventually kill what we have. And I won't let Blaine take anything else from me."

Stone was in a fantastic mood, despite the fact that Gray's contact had no leads on how to kill the media circus or identify who had broken into Piper's place. None of that mattered when he walked through his front door to find her standing at his windows, holding a glass of wine and staring out across the city.

She belonged there and if he had anything to say about it, she'd be staying. And not simply because her place was dangerous.

Stalking across the room, he barely paused to toss his keys into the bowl on the entrance table before wrapping his arms around her from behind and pulling her into his body. Piper relaxed into his hold, resting her head on his shoulder as she twisted so she could gift him with a soft smile. "How'd your meeting go? I assume everything turned out okay since you're here and not back in prison."

"Yes, smart-ass." Stone's hold tightened as he grinned down at her. "My meeting was fine. My parole officer is pushing me to make a decision about what I want to do since technically I should have employment. My situation is unique, but he's still concerned I don't have a purpose."

Piper laughed. "The man really doesn't know you, does he?"

"Not so much."

"Although, I suppose he isn't wrong since you've been out less than two weeks and have already broken one of the major rules of your release."

Stone leaned down and sealed his mouth to hers, pulling them both deep for several seconds before whispering against her lips, "Shh, that's our secret."

"Mmm," she murmured back. "I'll add it to the list."

Her words had Stone pulling away. "What's that supposed to mean?"

"Nothing. I made dinner. Wasn't sure when you'd be home so it's keeping warm in the oven."

Stone decided to let Piper's comment pass. He really wasn't in the mood to fight, not after the last few amazing days they'd shared. Together, they pulled down plates, finished dinner prep and settled in to share a meal. They fell into the easy pattern they'd developed on the island, perfect and comfortable.

Closing up the apartment for the night, Stone grasped Piper's hand and led her slowly into the bedroom. The moment felt pure and right. Like they'd been together this way for years instead of for days. Slowly, Stone undressed her, savoring each inch of skin. The way Piper stretched into his touch, chasing after more. The feel of her hands running over his body, the heat of her mouth as she rained kisses over him.

Sex with Piper was always good, but almost better tonight was curling up beside her, tucking her into his body and falling into a deep sleep with her next to him.

The next morning was easy and relaxed. They fell into an unspoken routine, getting ready for the day and sharing space. After Piper cooked breakfast and Stone cleaned up the kitchen, they headed out to Piper's place so she could pick up some more things.

Stone couldn't even remember what they talked about on the drive over. It didn't matter. What did matter was the happiness filling his chest. Happiness that if you'd asked him several months ago, he would have said he'd never have the opportunity to experience. Especially with her.

That happiness was shattered twenty minutes later.

Stone was sitting at Piper's kitchen table, a steaming mug of coffee in front of him, while she packed a bag in her bedroom.

He was in the middle of composing a text to Gray when her front door flew open, bouncing off the wall with a bang loud enough to be a gunshot.

Stone vaulted up from the table, coffee spilling across the surface and dripping off onto the floor. Down the hallway, he heard Piper's startled yelp. He should have had a weapon handy. Given everything going on, why hadn't he been prepared?

All these thoughts rampaged through his mind. His heart nearly bruised the back side of his ribs.

And nothing inside him settled when he realized Morgan was slamming through Piper's front door. Not when the man's expression looked like his child had just been murdered again.

Rounding the table, Stone tried to cut him off. He had no idea what was going on, but his assumption was that it had something to do with him. Maybe Stone's relationship with Piper?

What else could send Morgan into such a frenzy?

But Stone's hand pressed against Morgan's chest barely slowed him down. Like a bulldozer, the older man simply tried to run right over him. Morgan was on a mission and only stopped when Piper appeared in the doorway.

Stone knew the minute she came in, not just because Morgan stopped fighting. He always knew when Piper entered any room.

"Is it true?" Morgan wheezed, his voice hard and utterly destroyed.

The question was clearly directed at Piper, but Stone had no intention of letting her take the brunt of whatever was going down.

"Listen, man, I don't blame you for being upset. But Piper and I have cared about each other for a very long time."

Morgan's head jerked sideways, his gaze scraping across Stone's face with wild eyes. "Upset? I'm more than upset, Stone. I'm devastated that Piper's lived alone with this for ten years."

Okay, Stone was obviously missing something.

Confusion had the pressure he'd applied to Morgan's chest slackening. Taking advantage, Piper's stepfather scooted around Stone and stalked across the room to where she was rooted to the floor. Wrapping his arms around her, Morgan pulled her tight against his body, the hug so hard her toes lifted off the floor.

Burying his face in her hair, Stone watched as the man murmured, "I'm so sorry," against her head and simply held her, rocking back and forth as if she were a child. His child.

Stone stood, helpless, as Piper simply crumpled. She collapsed into Morgan's hold, letting him take her full weight. After several seconds, she mumbled, "How did you find out?"

"How did he find out?" Piper's mom's shrill voice punched through the room. Stone had been aware of her presence, but until that moment she'd simply been a quiet bystander.

Stalking across to them, she thrust a tablet into Piper's face. "What did you think was going to happen?"

Fourteen

Piper grasped her mother's wrist, holding the screen steady so she could actually read the bold words. The minute she did, her stomach dropped to her toes.

Rapist Stepbrother Murdered by Billionaire Boyfriend

Eyes racing, Piper scanned the text of the article. And the more she read the more she wanted to throw up. The story contained details only a few people knew—her, Stone and… Carina.

Holy hell, her best friend had sold her out.

As if that realization wasn't devastating enough, she didn't have time to deal with the fallout of that discovery. Not with her wrecked stepfather and wild mother in front of her.

Grasping her by the arms, Morgan pulled Piper's full attention back to him. Bending at the knees, he stared deep into her eyes. "Is it true?"

Piper swallowed. Tears welled in her eyes, but she refused to let them fall. She'd cried enough about what happened.

"Yes."

His expression crumpled and his grip on her tightened to the point of pain. But it was clear the pinch she was feeling was nothing compared to the anguish consuming him. Piper could see it, filling his gaze in a way that made her chest tight.

She'd had ten years to deal with the reality of what had happened to her. He'd only had a few minutes.

"Piper, I know it's not enough, but I'm eternally sorry for what Blaine did to you."

"It's not your fault."

"It is. It was my responsibility to protect you. You're my daughter and have been since the day I met you. I knew Blaine wasn't quite right, but never could I have imagined him capable of something so heinous."

Piper shook her head. "Blaine was a master at showing people what he wanted them to see."

"I'm learning that."

A noise caught Piper's attention. She jerked her head in time to see Stone tossing the tablet her mother had been holding onto her kitchen table. His gaze swept across them both, cold, hard and dead in a way that had icy panic swallowing her.

Oh, no.

She opened her mouth to explain to him about her conversation with Carina, but her stepfather stepped between them, interrupting. "Thank you for protecting her when I didn't."

It was a simple statement, but shot straight to her core. Gratitude, devastation, anger and hope. She didn't think her emotions could get any more tangled until Stone responded, "I loved her and would do anything to protect her."

"I know," Morgan responded.

Piper's entire body went red-hot before blanching cold again. Across her stepfather's shoulder, Stone's dead gaze swept over her from head to toe. Then, with her heart in her throat, Piper watched him turn and walk out her front door.

Without a word.

It was clear, without knowing of her conversation with Carina, Stone thought she was directly responsible for the details hitting the media.

He was doing it again. Shutting her out and cutting himself off. Without giving her a chance to explain. Without even the courtesy of a conversation.

No, she wasn't going to accept that this time.

Before, she'd been a scared, damaged girl who hadn't known how to fight for what she wanted. Now she was a strong woman, certain about what she wanted and determined enough to do whatever it took to get that.

And what she wanted was Stone in her life.

He might not understand—or forgive her—for

making the mistake of trusting Carina, but she wasn't going to let him simply walk away from her believing she'd purposely betrayed him.

But before she could move to follow Stone, her mother stepped right into her line of sight, cutting off her path to the door. Piper braced herself for a confrontation. Being an outsider to Morgan's social circle, her mother had always been protective of her reputation, and Piper's by association. The negative media attention surrounding Blaine's death had nearly sent her into a tailspin, which had been difficult for Piper to watch. It added to the guilt she'd already been carrying.

But instead of hysterics or accusation, her mother stared at her with watery, pain-filled eyes. Her gaze bounced from Piper to Morgan, still standing behind her, before her mother whispered, "I'm so sorry, Piper. Why didn't you tell us?"

Shaking her head, Piper swallowed the lump in her throat and tried to find the right words to explain. "I was afraid."

"Afraid of my reaction?" Morgan asked, stepping beside Piper.

"He was your son. Why would you believe me?"

Morgan grasped her hand, squeezing. "And you're my daughter."

The lump grew. "It all happened so fast. I was in shock. Devastated. Broken. Stone told me to leave that night, tell no one what had happened, and I was so numb I didn't even question why."

"You did what he said," her mother murmured.

Piper closed her eyes, reliving those first few days. They were a fog, but she distinctly remembered the devastating push and pull of trying to decide what to do. Wishing she had Stone to talk to.

"Blaine was gone. Stone was in jail and bringing up the truth at that point seemed…futile. By the time I realized what he was doing he'd pleaded guilty, gotten a reduced sentence and was already on his way to prison. What would it have changed?"

"Nothing. And everything." Reaching out, Morgan wrapped his arms around Piper. "It would have helped us understand. And you wouldn't have had to deal with this on your own for so long."

Her mother joined them, wrapping her arms around both of them. Sandwiched between her parents, Piper sagged into the shelter of their love and support.

She'd worked hard to heal herself over the last ten years. But there was no replacement for that kind of acceptance and comfort. Piper whispered, "I love you both."

A weight that had initially lessened when she shared the truth with Carina became even lighter knowing she was no longer keeping this heavy secret from her parents.

But she couldn't fully put the burden down. Not until she fixed things with Stone.

Stone was so angry he couldn't see straight.

He didn't remember driving back to his place, but he definitely was aware when he walked through the front door, snatched up the first thing he could find—a potted plant—and threw it against the wall.

The loud bang and shower of potting soil were hardly cathartic. In fact, the mangled pile of leaves and dirt reminded him of the mess his life had just crumbled into.

The headline kept scrolling across his mind, the one word highlighted in red.

Murderer.

Certainly, he'd already carried that label. But Piper hadn't. Now her life would forever be linked with Blaine's death. With the stain on his own soul. How could they move forward and build a life together when it would forever be tainted with what he'd done?

They didn't have a future. He'd known that from the moment he'd killed Blaine, but the last few days had made him forget. Had almost convinced him they could move past it all. But now…

He'd explained to her why keeping silent was important to him, but it didn't matter. Or not enough to outweigh her damn idea of setting them free. Something he could never be.

Didn't she realize now neither of them would ever be free?

At her place, Stone had felt the familiar coldness he'd had to adopt in prison slowly crystallizing through his body again.

And he'd hated it.

The only way he'd been able to do what needed to be done for the last ten years was to distance himself. To find a deep, dark well of indifference. It had accompanied him home, and right into that damn library where she'd cracked the protective exterior.

As he'd walked out her door, Stone embraced the familiar sensation. Welcomed it. He was going to need the numbness in order to get through the next days, weeks…hell, years without her.

But the minute he'd stepped inside his home to see the sweater she'd draped over one of his kitchen chairs, that numbness had fled, leaving him with the ache of grief and pain. And a shattered pot.

Stone had no idea how long he stood there, staring at the mess. But the next coherent thought was the realization someone had just walked in his front door. Only a handful of people were on the list downstairs to be let up. And even fewer had the code to his front door.

But he'd given it to Piper just this morning.

Stone didn't bother turning around. He knew it was her the minute she crossed into the room. Even if the mingled scents of spice and vanilla hadn't teased him, he'd have known. Just as he was aware when she stopped several feet away from him.

"Stone."

A part of him wanted to ignore her, like a kid with his head stuck under the blanket to protect from closet monsters. But he hadn't been a kid in a long time. And part of him knew there was no way she'd let him walk away without a confrontation.

Maybe better now than later.

Spinning slowly on his heel, Stone faced her. Even

with disheveled hair and a tear-ravaged face, she was so beautiful. Would always be that way to him.

The anguish in her gaze was real. She watched him warily, as if she expected him to go off like a pinless hand grenade.

None of that changed anything for him.

With all her talk of honesty, she'd made certain he could never distance himself—and them—from what had happened. And part of him felt betrayed because she obviously didn't understand.

"There's nothing left to say, Piper. You said it already. To someone else."

"I didn't," she said, shaking her head.

"I read the article. I didn't speak with anyone and considering the details, that just leaves you. Tell me the info in that piece didn't come from you."

Piper opened her mouth, but shut it again. Guilt clouded her expression, admitting what she couldn't seem to find the nerve to say. He'd have respected her more if she'd simply owned what she'd done and told him to go to hell.

"It's not what you think."

Stone shook his head and turned to walk away from her again. Why was it getting harder and harder each time he had to do it?

But this time, he didn't get two steps before Piper's hands grasped his arms and jerked him to a stop. She spun him around and, before he could draw a breath, plastered her mouth to his.

The kiss was hard and deep. All-consuming.

Stone couldn't stop his body from responding. From wanting her. From betraying him.

Desperation filled the connection, hers and his. Stone tried to pull back, but she wouldn't let him. And then he simply gave in. Stone let every speck of the anger and torment fuel him. He grasped Piper's arms, pulling her up onto her toes and jerking her harshly into his body.

He devoured her. His hands tore at her clothing, trying to find skin. Stone heard a seam rip, but didn't care.

Until she pushed at him. Her hands scrabbled against his chest, fighting for purchase and space. "Stone, stop."

Even through his anger and heartache that was all he needed to pull back.

But Piper didn't let him get far. She grasped his face and held him still, bringing her nose inches from his own. Staring into his eyes with those pale blue pools that always slayed him.

"I didn't talk to Madelyn Black."

Her statement was harsh and definite, leaving no room for him to question the truth behind it. Then she continued, "Yesterday, Carina came over while you were gone and I *did* tell her what happened. Not only did she deserve to know the truth about what happened to her fiancé, I realized I had no right to push you to tell the world about what happened when I wasn't willing to share the truth with the people closest to me. There was no way for me to know she'd turn around and sell the story to a reporter, which is my assumption about what happened."

Piper's words sank into his brain. Hope spread, warm and deep, through the center of his chest. She hadn't spoken to the media. Yes, she'd shared with Carina, which didn't make him happy but...she hadn't ignored his wishes either.

"I love you. I might not understand or agree with your stance on keeping the truth private, but I respect you enough to allow you to make that decision. However, you have no right to ask that I keep the truth from the people in my life that deserve to know. I took a risk, admittedly, a bad one, but at the time I felt comfortable with the decision." Her grip on his jaw tightened. "I'm so, so sorry my decision caused you pain and will make your life more difficult."

Stone stared deep into Piper's eyes. The love she felt for him was there, staring back at him.

"Don't you get it? I'm not worried about my life being difficult, Piper. I'd do anything to save you from being tainted by what I did."

Piper's eyebrows slammed together in irritation and disbelief. "Tainted by what you did? Stone, I was saved by what you did. I'm grateful for what you did."

Her grip on him tightened. "I wish it hadn't happened this way, but I'm glad the secret no longer has any hold over either of us. The world will finally understand what a wonderful man you are. Will recognize the sacrifice you made in order to protect me."

She moved closer, pressing the warmth of her body against his. Until that moment, he hadn't realized how cold he'd become.

"You're caring and selfless, Stone. You place the needs of everyone around you before your own. And I'm so lucky to have you in my life."

Pushing onto her toes, Piper fused her mouth with his for several seconds. The heat of her kiss melted through him before she abruptly pulled back. "And, just so you know, I'm not going to let you walk away from me again. It's my turn to fight for you."

Stone gripped her hands. For a brief moment, every terrible thing he'd ever done flashed through his mind. Blaine, prison, dangerous, despicable things that had scarred his soul and left him certain he'd never deserve anyone, least of all her. He should push her away.

But he couldn't.

Not when she was standing in front of him, staring up with her calm, steady, determined gaze. She was stubborn enough to do exactly as she threatened. And he didn't want to let her go.

Wasn't sure he had it in him to do it again.

She obviously didn't blame him or hold what had happened against him. In fact, instead of seeing him as a monster, she viewed him as a savior. She'd forgiven him for what happened, maybe it was time he forgave himself.

Dipping down, Stone sealed his mouth with hers. Unlike before, this kiss held nothing but love and light. And it tugged at him to let go and sink into the connection they shared.

But before he could do that, he needed to clear up a few things.

"I'm sorry for doubting you. The thought of you doing the one thing I asked you not to…gutted me in a way that left me hollow and numb. Piper, very few things scare me because very few things have the ability to hurt me. You can."

She shook her head, opening her mouth to argue, but he continued over her, cutting off the protest.

"I know you wouldn't. Not intentionally anyway. I'll never be happy that your pain has been splashed all over the media for people to dissect and judge. But I know you're strong. Strong enough to handle the scrutiny."

Her lips tipped up in a half smile. "Yes, yes I am."

"And you have plenty of people around you willing to support you. Not just me."

"You're right. It hurts that the woman I thought was my best friend has betrayed me. But I have so many other people who love me and will help me get through this. I know you're not happy, but I think the truth being out will help us both move forward with our lives. With each other. The one thing that had the potential to come between us is gone."

It was Stone's turn to flash her a soft smile. "Now we're free to just love each other and build a life together."

Her hands rubbed across his chest. "Exactly."

Pressing his forehead to hers, Stone breathed

deeply, letting the scent of her settle into his soul. Pulling back, he whispered, "I've loved you for so long. Over the years that connection has changed and grown. Intensified. Piper, you're my world, and I don't want to think about life without you."

A bright smile flashed across her face, lighting up her eyes and his heart. "Don't worry, I have no intention of letting you do life without me ever again. I love you, Stone. Not many people get to say the best day of their life happened at six, but mine did. Because it brought me you."

Epilogue

Several hours later, still curled up together in bed, Piper's phone rang. Morgan's name flashed across the screen. She didn't hesitate to answer. "Everything okay?"

"Everything's fine. I was calling to let you know I confronted Carina. She admitted to selling the story to Madelyn Black. And the photograph from the party. She also broke into your place, which wasn't difficult since you'd given her a key."

Having her assumption confirmed felt very anti-climactic. The truth didn't change a single thing, although maybe it did turn the lock on the doors she and Stone had both closed tonight.

"Apparently, she was tired of depending on your mother and me for everything. She wanted the money she would have had if she and Blaine had married and decided to use the information you gave her in order to get it."

Morgan's words filled Piper with sadness. How could she have been so unaware of Carina's unhappiness and dissatisfaction? She'd always thought they were close. Shared so much.

It was crushing to discover she'd been so wrong.

And it was tempting to blame herself for missing the signs. She was a psychologist for God's sake. Seeing behind people's words and actions to the underlying force behind them was her job.

After hanging up with Morgan, she recounted her conversation to Stone and shared her own complicated emotions. Typical Stone, his response was to tug a comfy sweatshirt over her head, pour her a glass of wine and curl up with her on the sofa as they settled into a movie on TV.

She was mellow and relaxed when Stone's phone rang. Piper wasn't really paying any attention to the conversation until she clued in that the person on the other end was the doorman from downstairs letting them know someone had stopped by.

Piper followed behind as Stone moved toward the front door. Opening it, she peeked around his wide shoulders to find a strange man standing in the doorway, a mischievous grin splitting his tanned face.

Stone's eyebrows beetled in confusion. "I didn't think you were supposed to be out for another six months."

With a smirk and a shrug the man responded,

"Good behavior," in a way that indicated the words were clearly a lie.

Stepping back, Stone swept his arm inside. "Piper, meet Finn DeLuca, the slipperiest bastard you'll ever meet."

* * * * *

Charming and wicked, Finn DeLuca doesn't steal for the riches. He does it for the rush. Or he used to, until Genevieve Reilly changes everything.

Look for The Devil's Bargain, *available October 2020 and Gray's story,* The Sinner's Secret, *coming November 2020!*

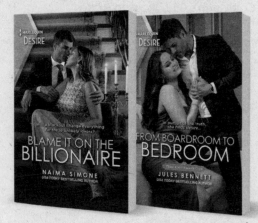

*A tempting new music venture reunites songwriter
Eden Voss with ex-boyfriend Blaine Woodson, a record
label executive. He wronged her in the past, so they vow
to keep things strictly business this time. But there is
nothing professional about the heat still between them…*

Read on for a sneak peek at
After Hours Redemption *by Kianna Alexander.*

Singing through the opening verse, she could feel the smile
coming over her face. Singing gave her a special kind of joy, a
feeling she didn't get from anything else. There was nothing quite
like opening her mouth and letting her voice soar.

She was rounding the second chorus when she noticed Blaine
standing in the open door to the booth. Surprised, and a bit
embarrassed, she stopped midnote.

His face filled with earnest admiration, he spoke into the
awkward silence. "Please, Eden. Don't stop."

Heat flared in her chest, and she could feel it rising into her
cheeks. "Blaine, I…"

"It's been so long since I've heard you sing." He took a step
closer. "I don't want it to be over yet."

Swallowing her nervousness, she picked up where she'd left
off. Now that he was in the room, the lyrics, about a secret romance
between two people with plenty of baggage, suddenly seemed
much more potent.

And personal.

Suddenly, this song, which she often sang in the shower or
while driving, simply because she found it catchy, became almost
autobiographical. Under the intense, watchful gaze of the man
she'd once loved, every word took on new meaning.

She sang the song to the end, then eased her fingertips away
from the keys.

Blaine burst into applause. "You've still got it, Eden."

"Thank you," she said, her tone softer than she'd intended. She looked away, reeling from the intimacy of the moment. Having him as a spectator to her impassioned singing felt too familiar, too reminiscent of a time she'd fought hard to forget.

"I'm not just gassing you up, either." His tone quiet, almost reverent, he took a few slow steps until he was right next to her. "I hear singing all day, every day. But I've never, ever come across another voice like yours."

She sucked in a breath, and his rich, woodsy cologne flooded her senses, threatening to undo her. Blowing the breath out, she struggled to find words to articulate her feelings. "I appreciate the compliment, Blaine. I really do. But…"

"But what?" He watched her intently. "Is something wrong?"

She tucked in her bottom lip. *How can I tell him that being this close to him ruins my concentration? That I can't focus on my work because all I want to do is climb him like a tree?*

"Eden?"

"I'm fine." She shifted on the stool, angling her face away from him in hopes that she might regain some of her faculties. His physical size, combined with his overt masculine energy, seemed to fill the space around her, making the booth feel even smaller than it actually was.

He reached out, his fingertips brushing lightly over her bare shoulder. "Are you sure?"

She trembled, reacting to the tingling sensation brought on by his electric touch. For a moment, she wanted him to continue, wanted to feel his kiss. Soon, though, common sense took over, and she shook her head. "Yes, Blaine. I'm positive."

Will Eden be able to maintain her resolve?

Don't miss what happens next in…
After Hours Redemption *by Kianna Alexander.*

Available October 2020 wherever
Harlequin Desire books and ebooks are sold.

Harlequin.com

Get 4 FREE REWARDS!

We'll send you 2 FREE Books plus 2 FREE Mystery Gifts.

Harlequin Desire® books transport you to the world of the American elite with juicy plot twists, delicious sensuality and intriguing scandal.

FREE Value Over **$20**

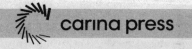
*At Dallas's iconic luxury department store, you can
feel good about indulging a little...or a lot. The staff is
proud of their store. If you're one of them, you're three
things: brilliant, boss and bomb.*

*Julia del Mar Ortiz moved to Texas with her boyfriend,
who ended up ditching her and running back to
New York after only a few weeks. Left with a massive—
by NYC standards, anyway—apartment and the job
opportunity of a lifetime, Julia is struggling...
except that's not completely true...*

Read on for a sneak preview of
Here to Stay
*by Adriana Herrera,
available now from Carina Press.*

He brought his cat to dinner.

I opened the door to my apartment and found Rocco holding the
little carrier we'd bought for Pulga at the pet store in one hand and
in the other he had a reusable shopping bag with what looked like
his contribution for dinner.

"Hey, I know you said she was uninvited." His eyebrows
dipped, obviously worried I'd be pissed at this plus-one situation.
I wanted to kiss him so bad, I was dizzy. "But whenever I tried to
leave the house, she started mewling really loud. I think she's still
dehydrated."

Boy, was I in over my head.

I smiled and tried not to let him see how his words had actually
turned me into a puddle of goo. "It's fine, since she's convalescent

and all, but once she's back in shape, she's banned from this apartment."

He gave a terse nod, still looking embarrassed. "Promise."

I waved him on, but before I could get another word in, my mom came out of my room in full "Dia de Fiesta" hair and makeup. Holidays that involved a meal meant my mother had to look like she was going to a red carpet somewhere. She was wearing an orange sheath dress with her long brown hair cascading over her shoulders and three-inch heels on her feet.

To have dinner in my cramped two-bedroom apartment.

"Rocco, you're here. *Qué bueno.*" She leaned over and kissed him on the cheek, then gestured toward the living room. "Julita, I'm so glad you invited him. We have too much food."

"Thank you for letting me join you." Rocco gave me the look that I'd been getting from my friends my entire life, that said, *Damn, your mom is hot.* It was not easy to shine whenever my mother was around, but we were still obligated to try.

I'd complied with a dark green wrap dress and a little bit of mascara and lip stain, but I was nowhere near as made-up as she was. Except now I wished I'd made more of an effort, and why was I comparing myself to my mom and why did I care what Rocco thought?

I was about to say something, anything, to get myself out of this mindfucky headspace when he walked into my living room and, as he'd done with my mom, bent his head and brushed a kiss against my cheek. As he pulled back, he looked at me appreciatively, his gaze caressing me from head to toe.

"You look beautiful." There was fluttering occurring inside me again, and for a second I really wished I could just push up and kiss him. Or punch him. God, I was a mess.

Don't miss what happens next…
Here to Stay *by Adriana Herrera*
available wherever Carina Press books
and ebooks are sold.

CarinaPress.com